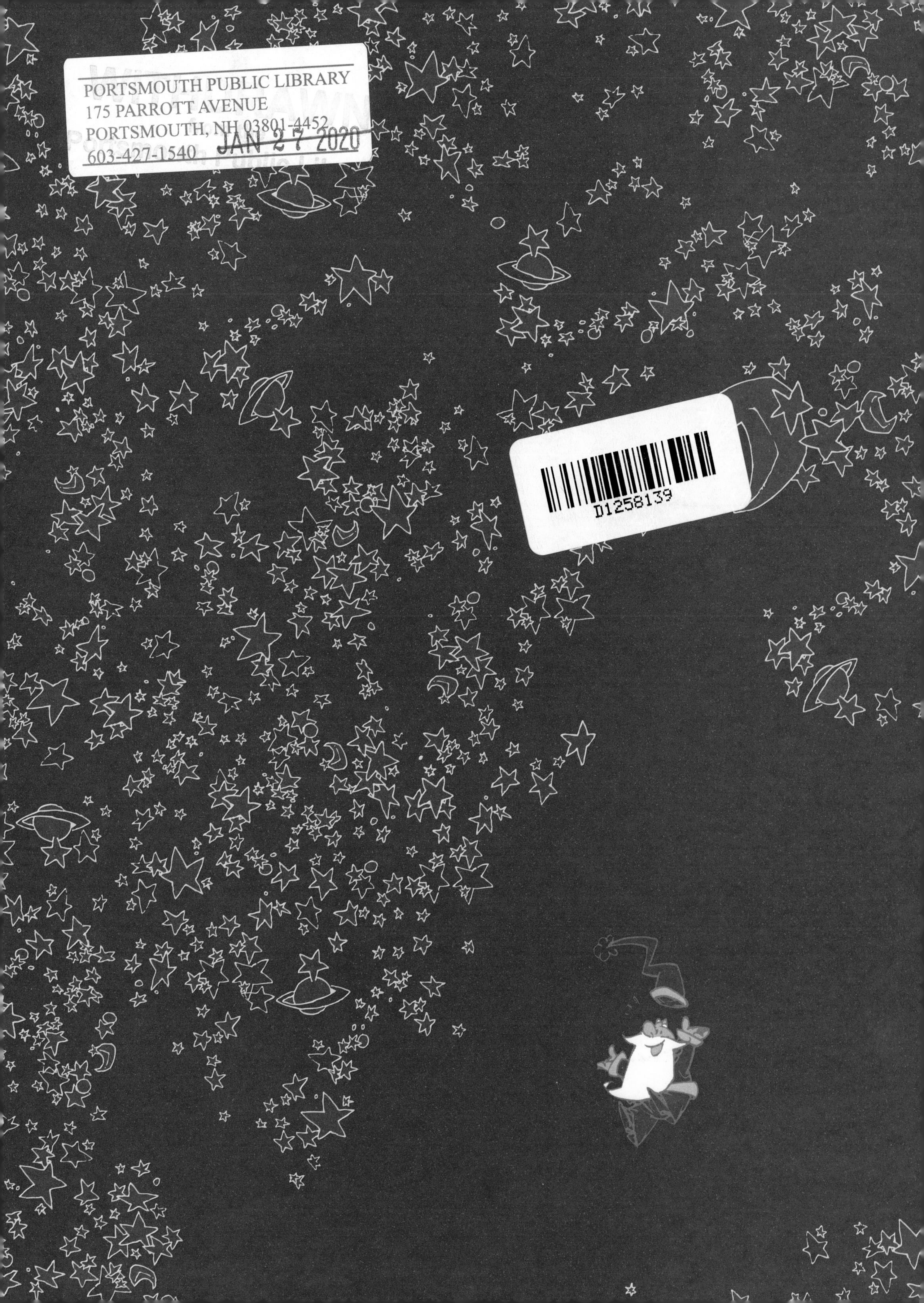

Happy Halloween,
Li'l Santa

Lewis Trondheim, story
Thierry Robin, art
Isabelle Busschaert, colors

ISBN 1-56163-361-5
© 2001 Dupuis
© 2003 NBM for the English translation
Library of Congress Control Number: 2003109738
Printed in Hong Kong

5   4   3   2   1

NANTIER · BEALL · MINOUSTCHINE
Publishing inc.
new york

We have over 200 graphic novels in print, write for our color catalog:
NBM, 555 8th Ave., Suite 1202, New York, NY 10018
www.nbmpublishing.com/tales

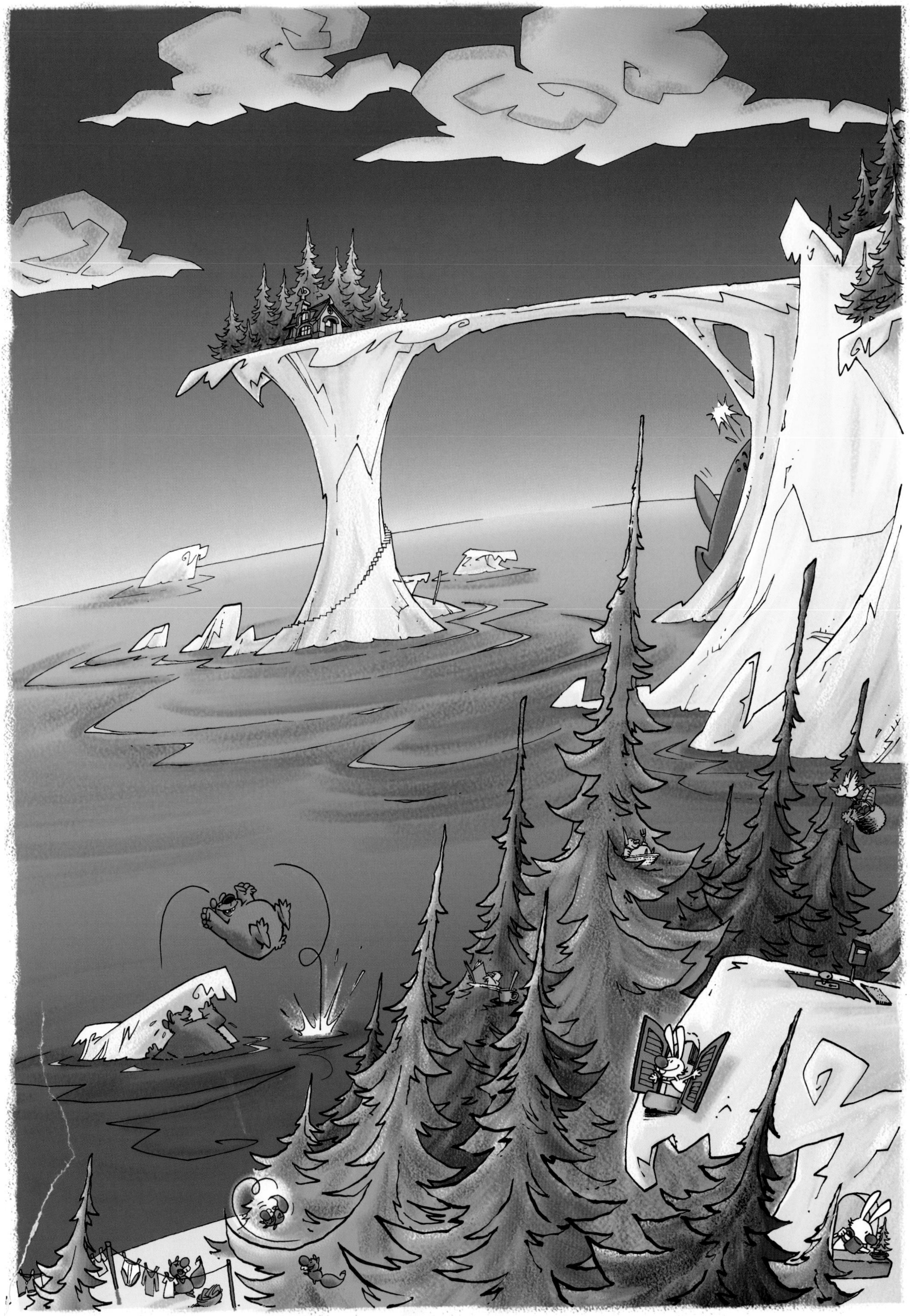

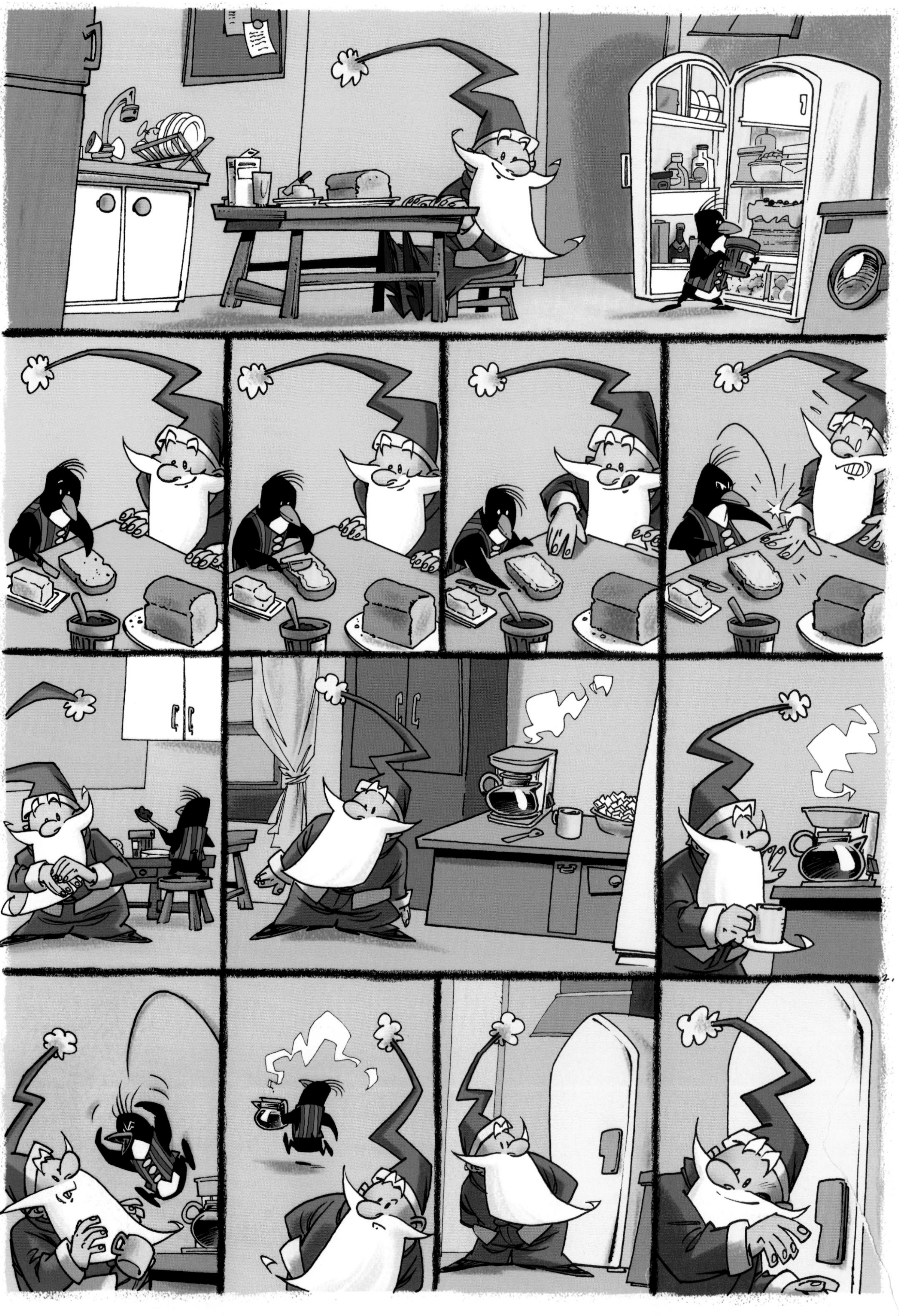

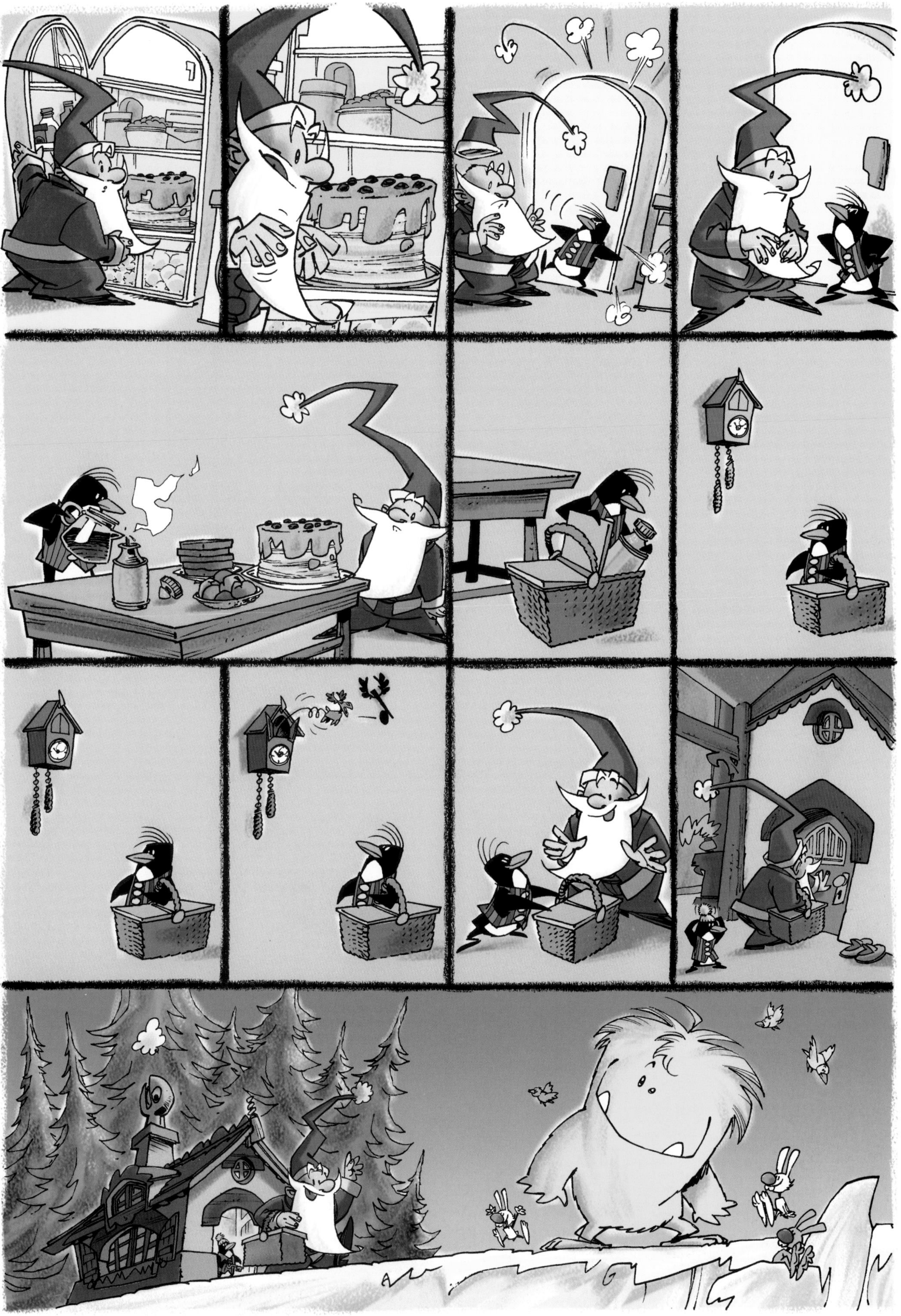

3.

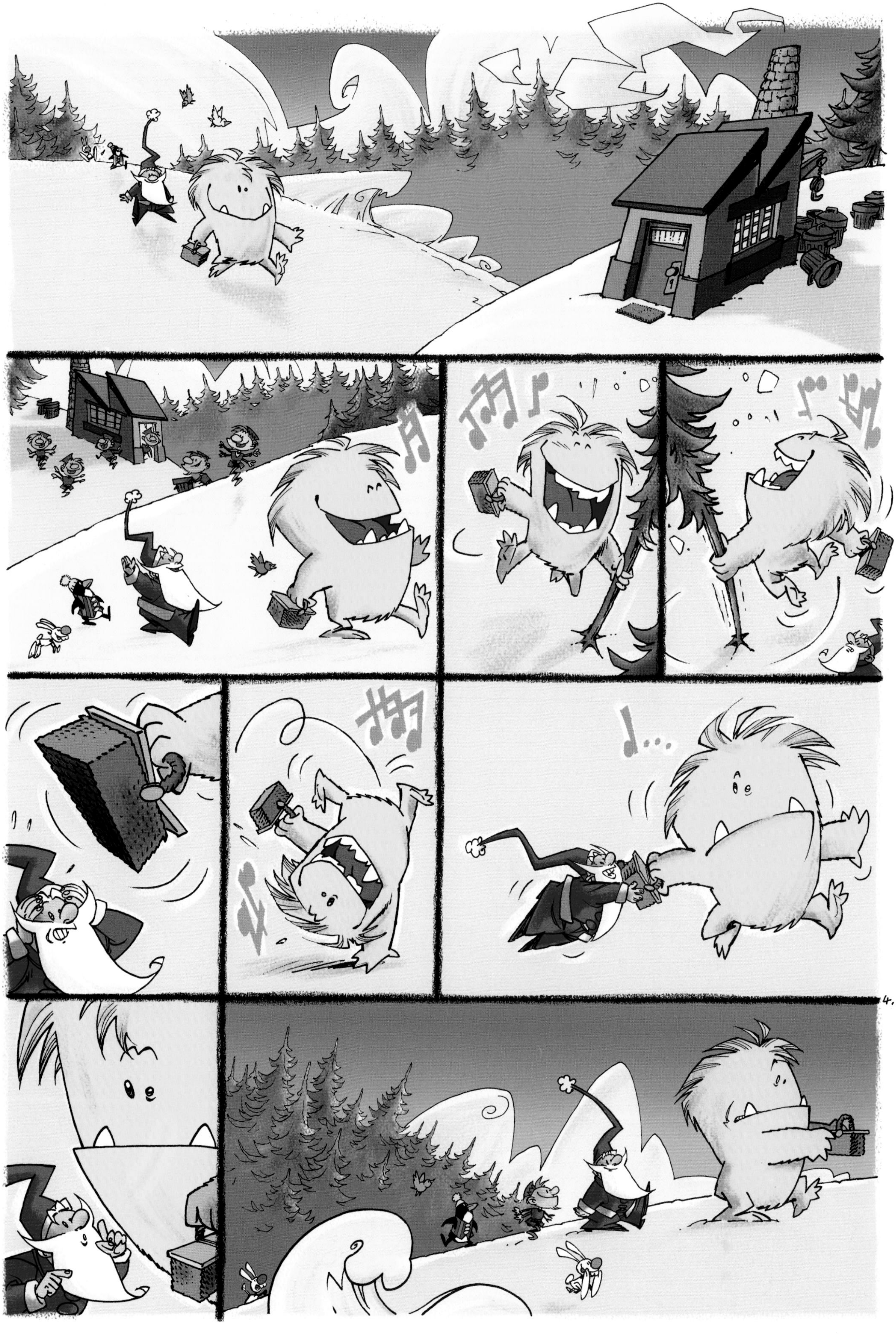

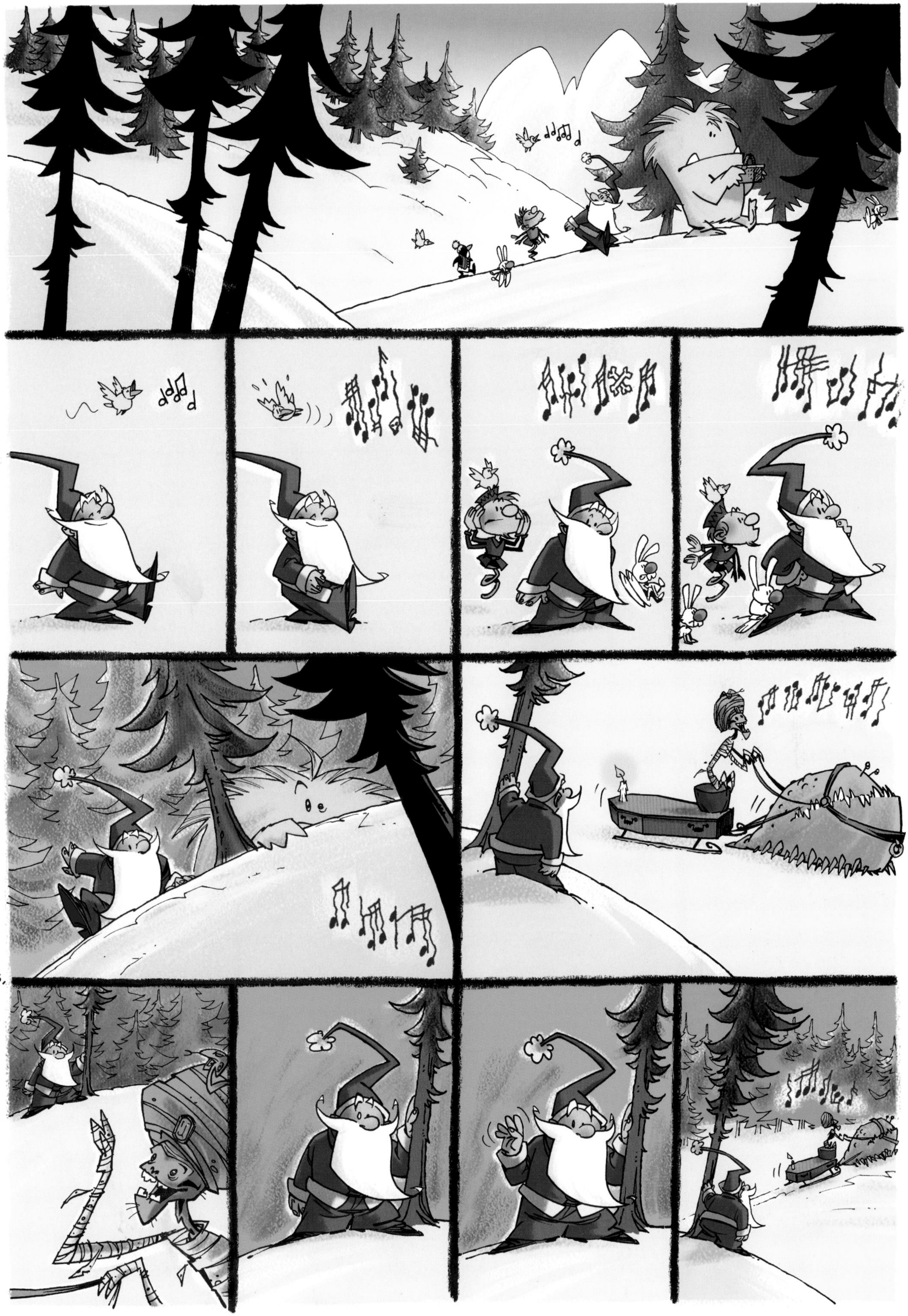

5,

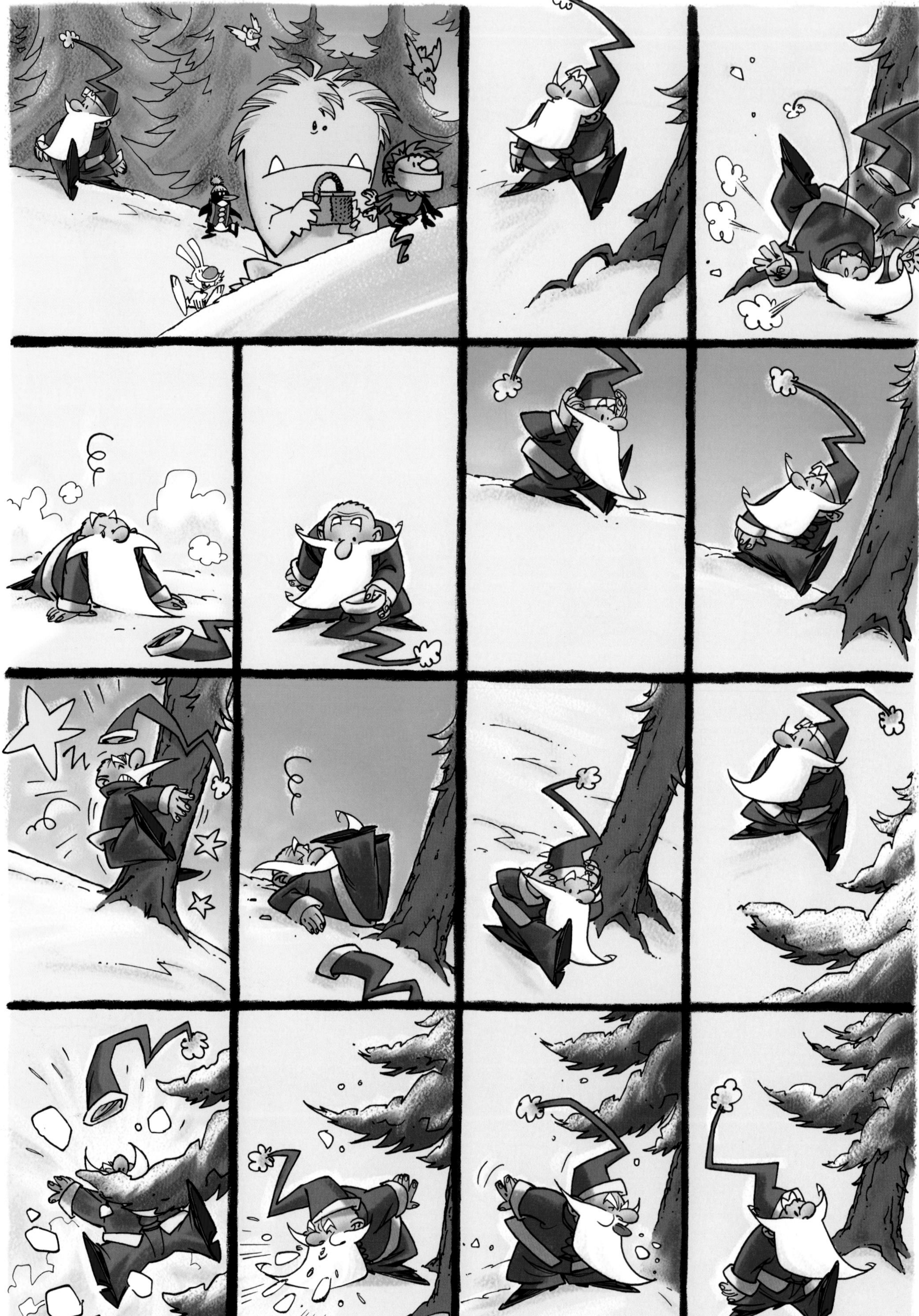

6.

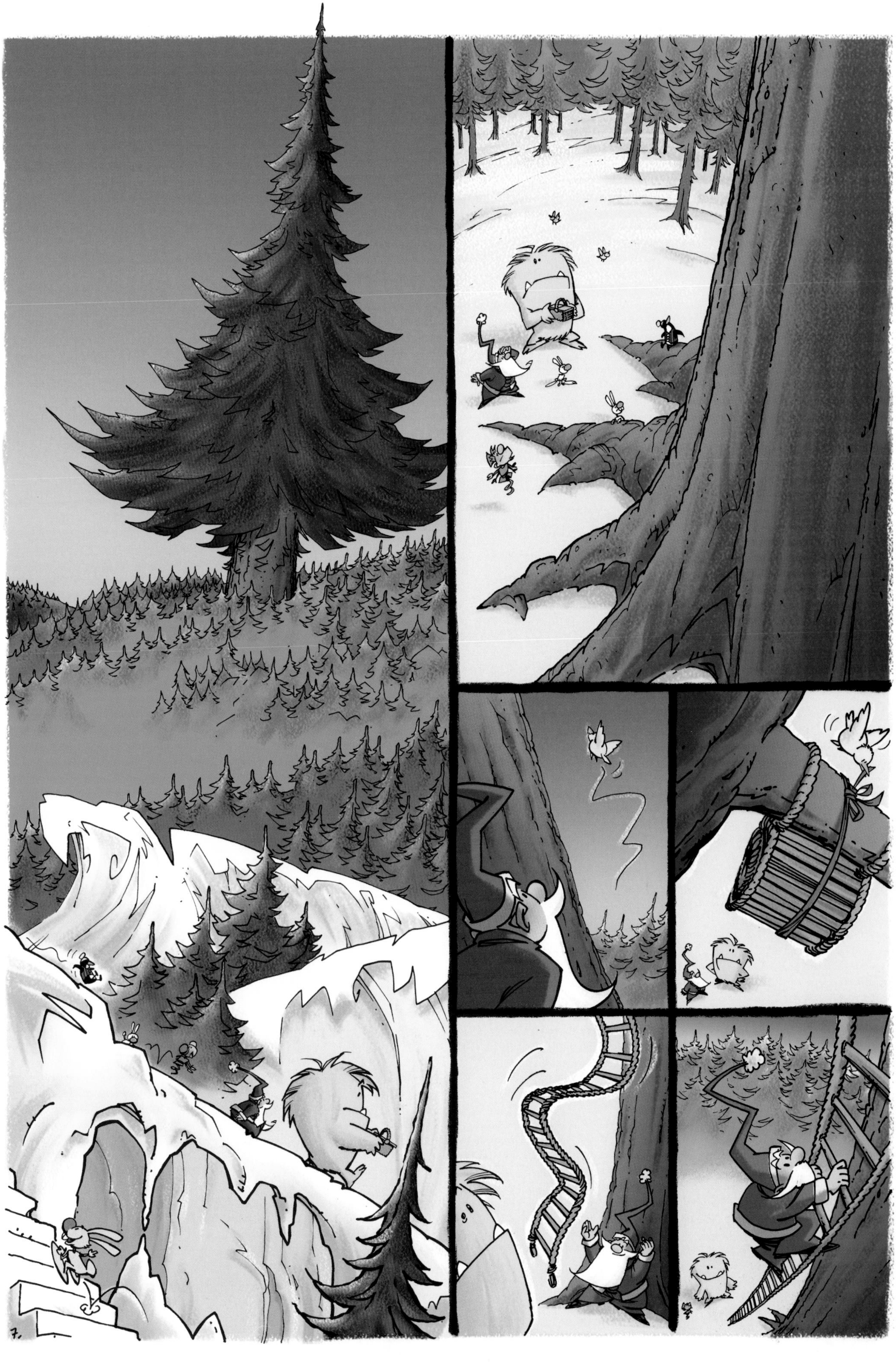

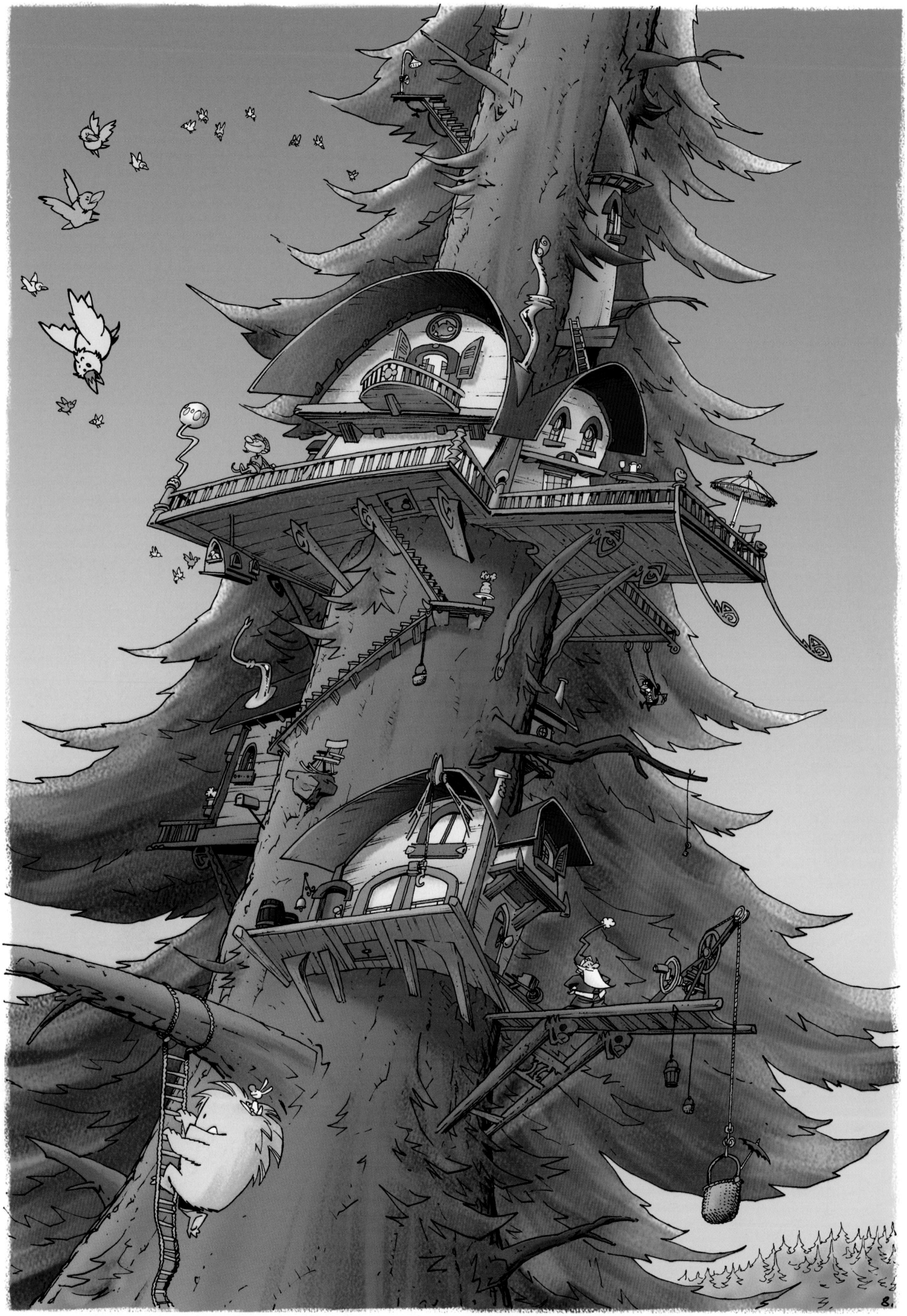

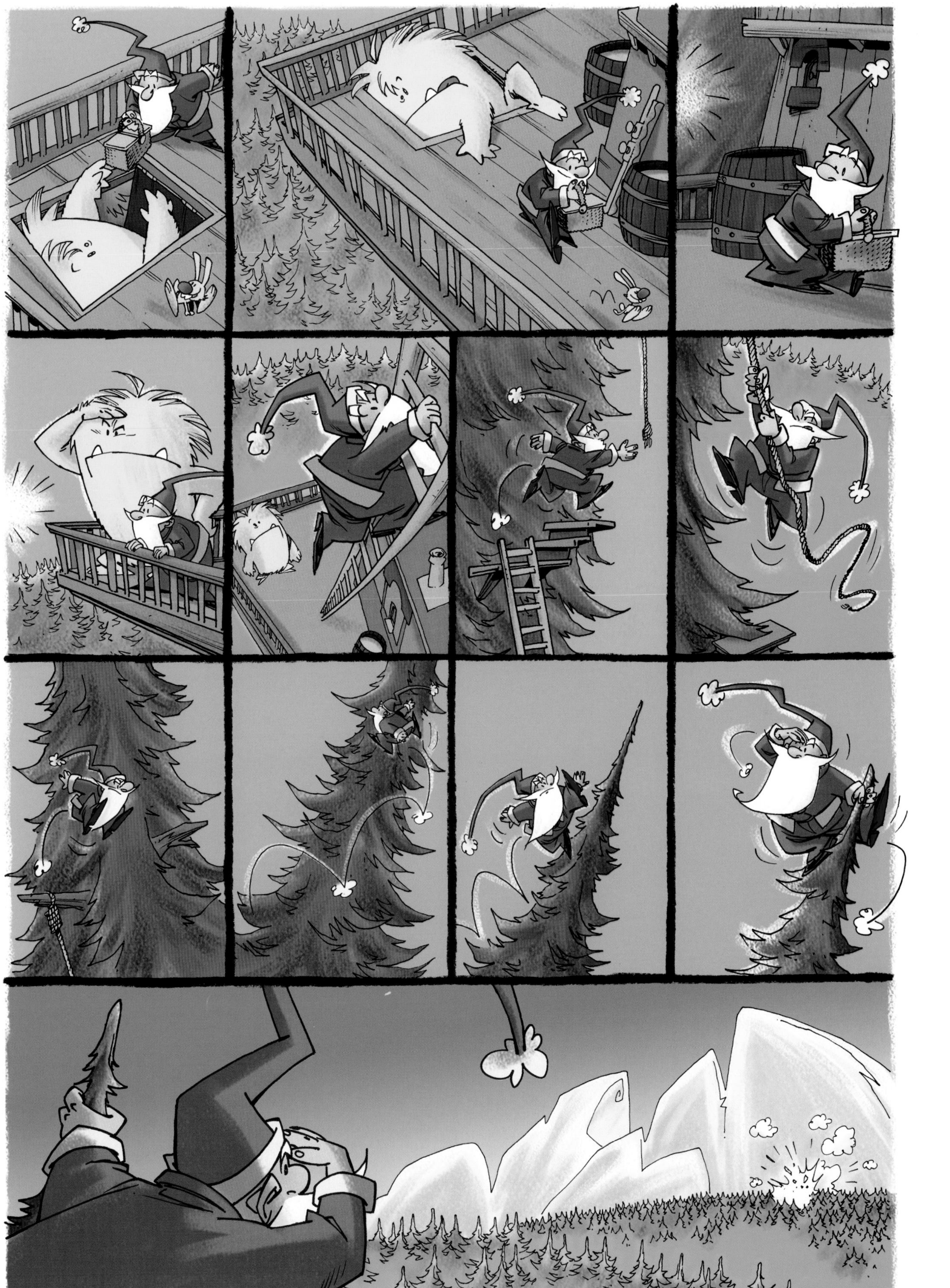

9.

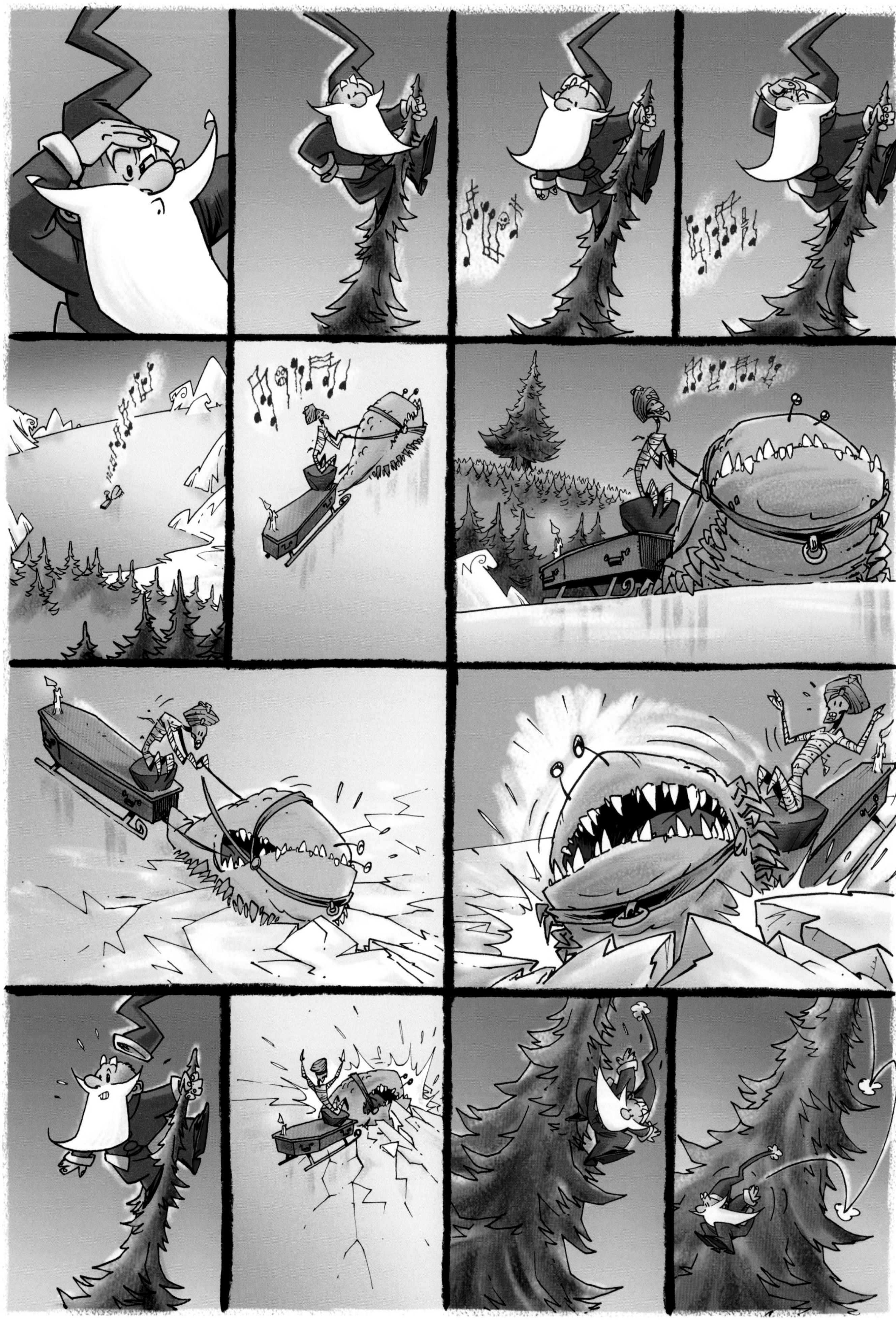

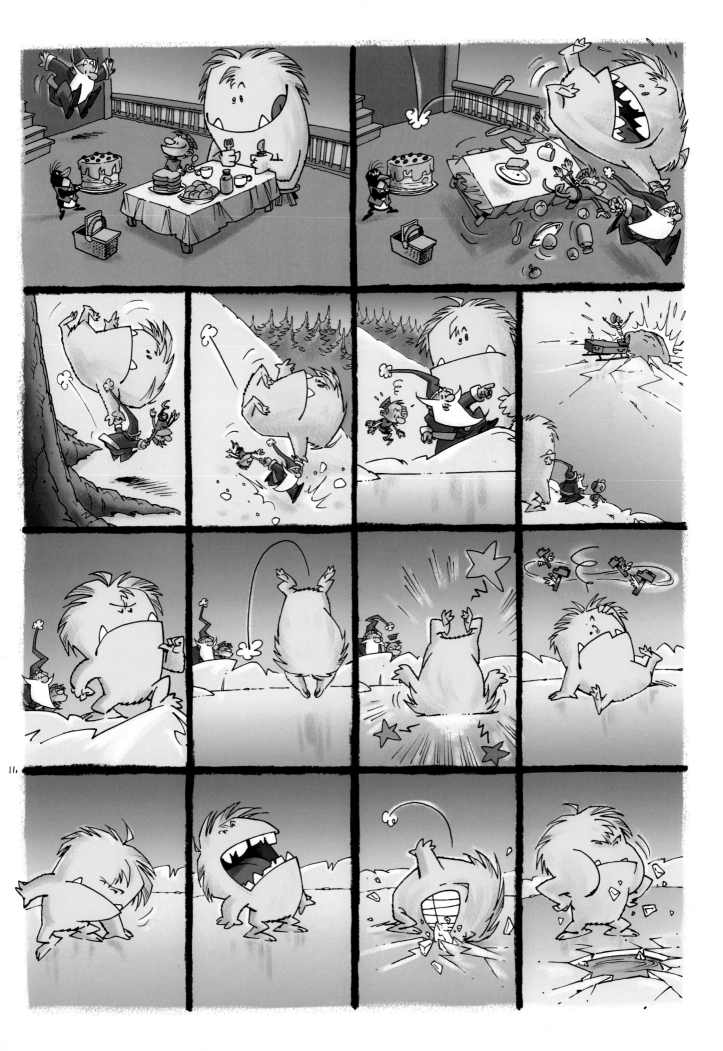

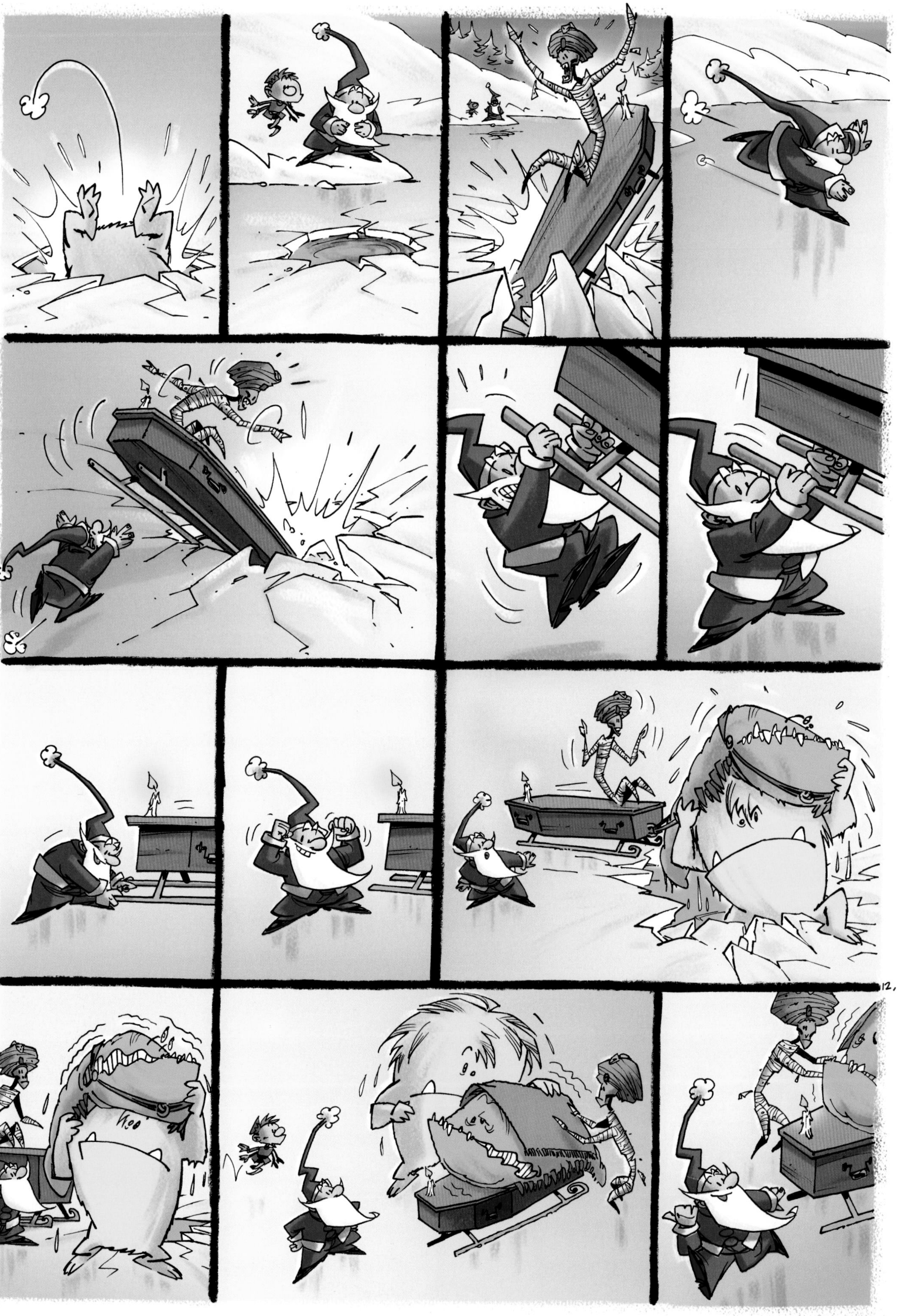
12,

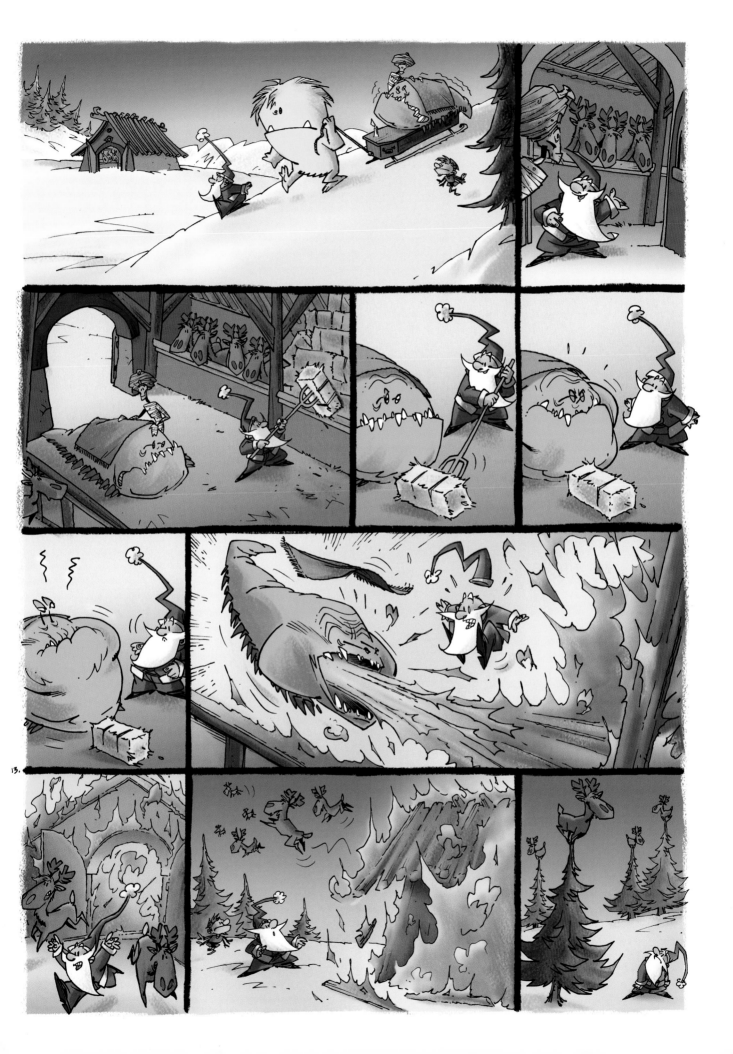

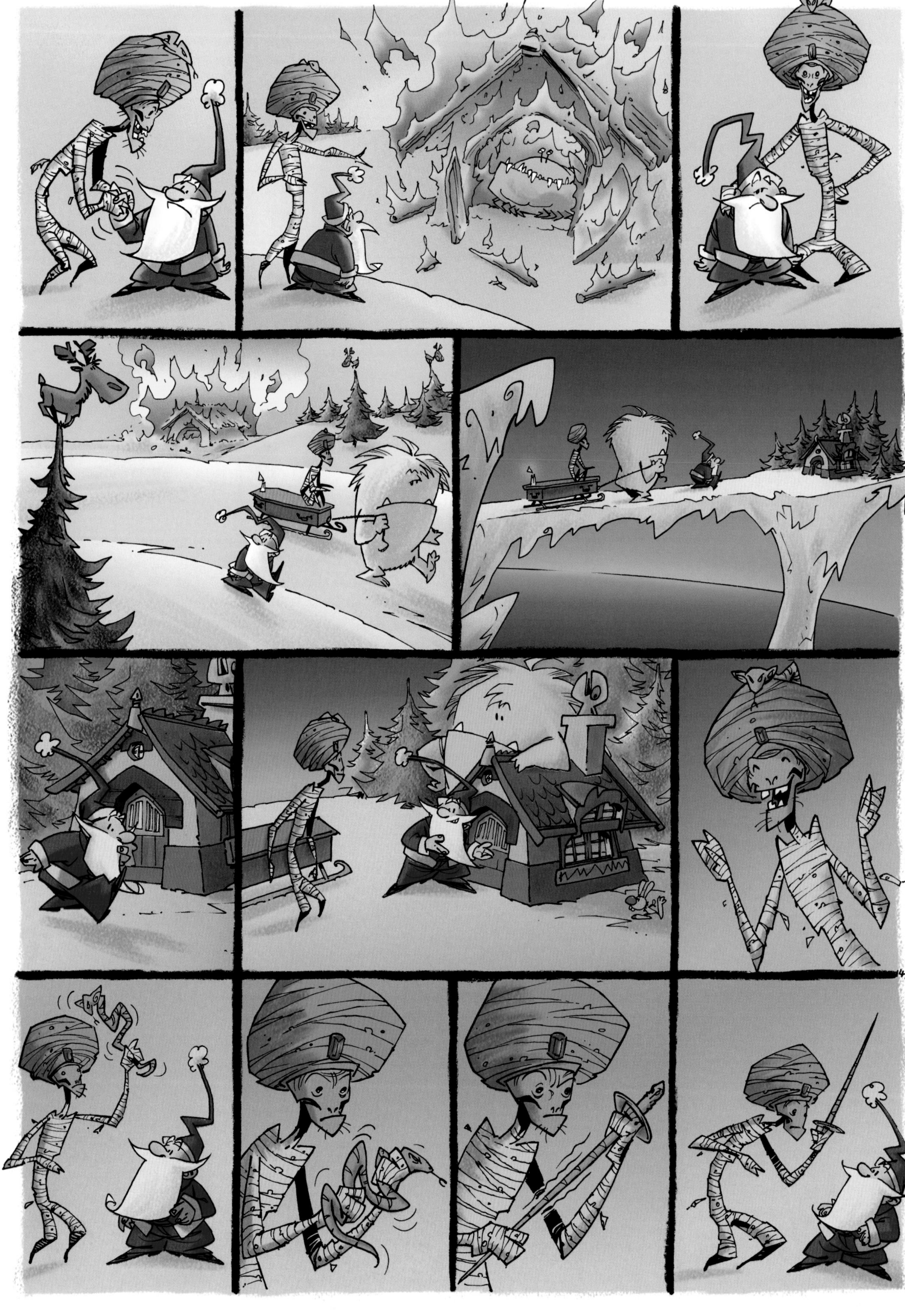

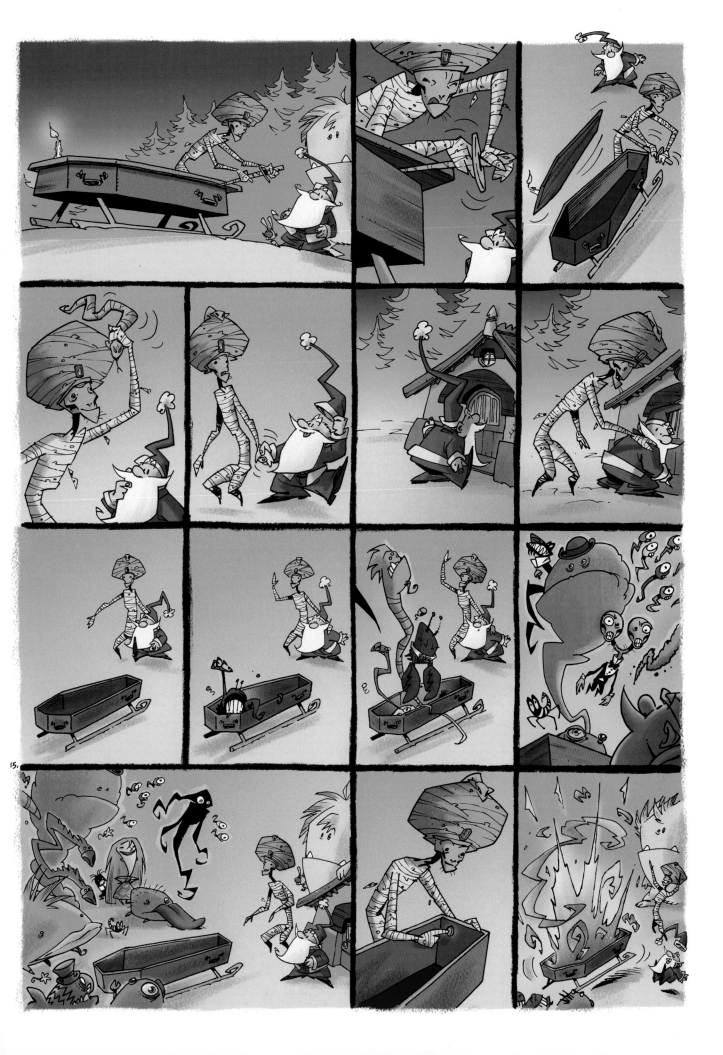

15.

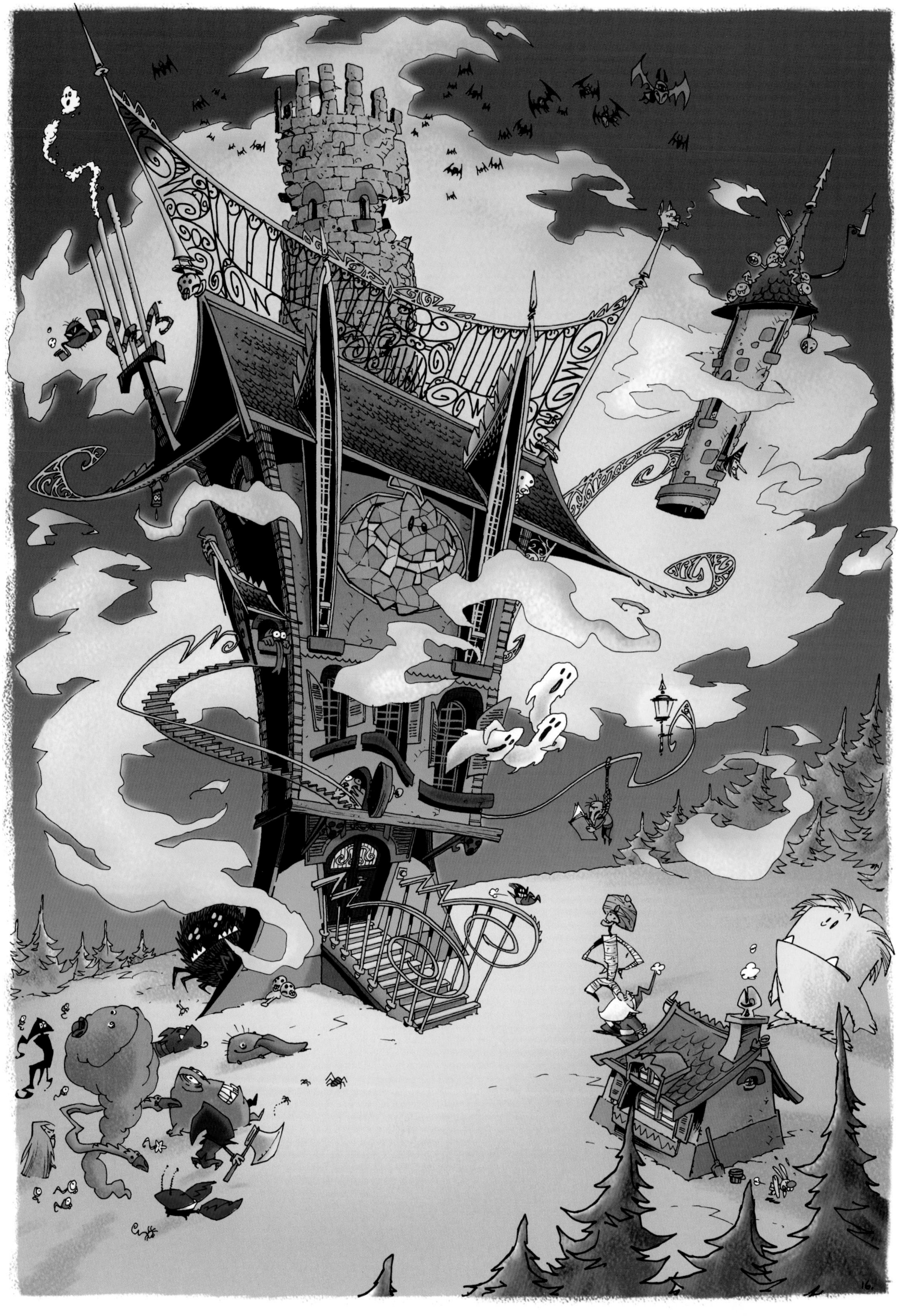
16.

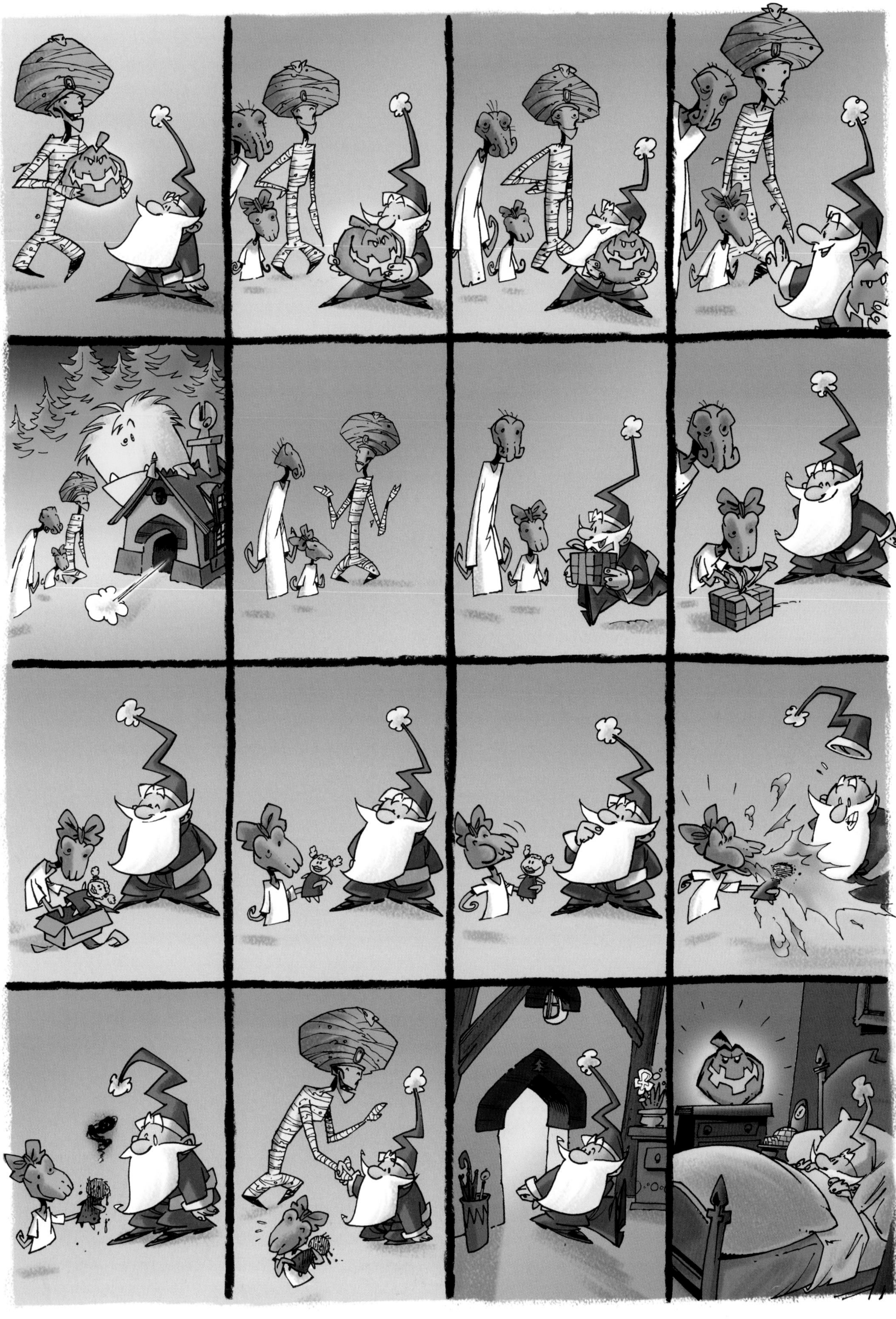

17.

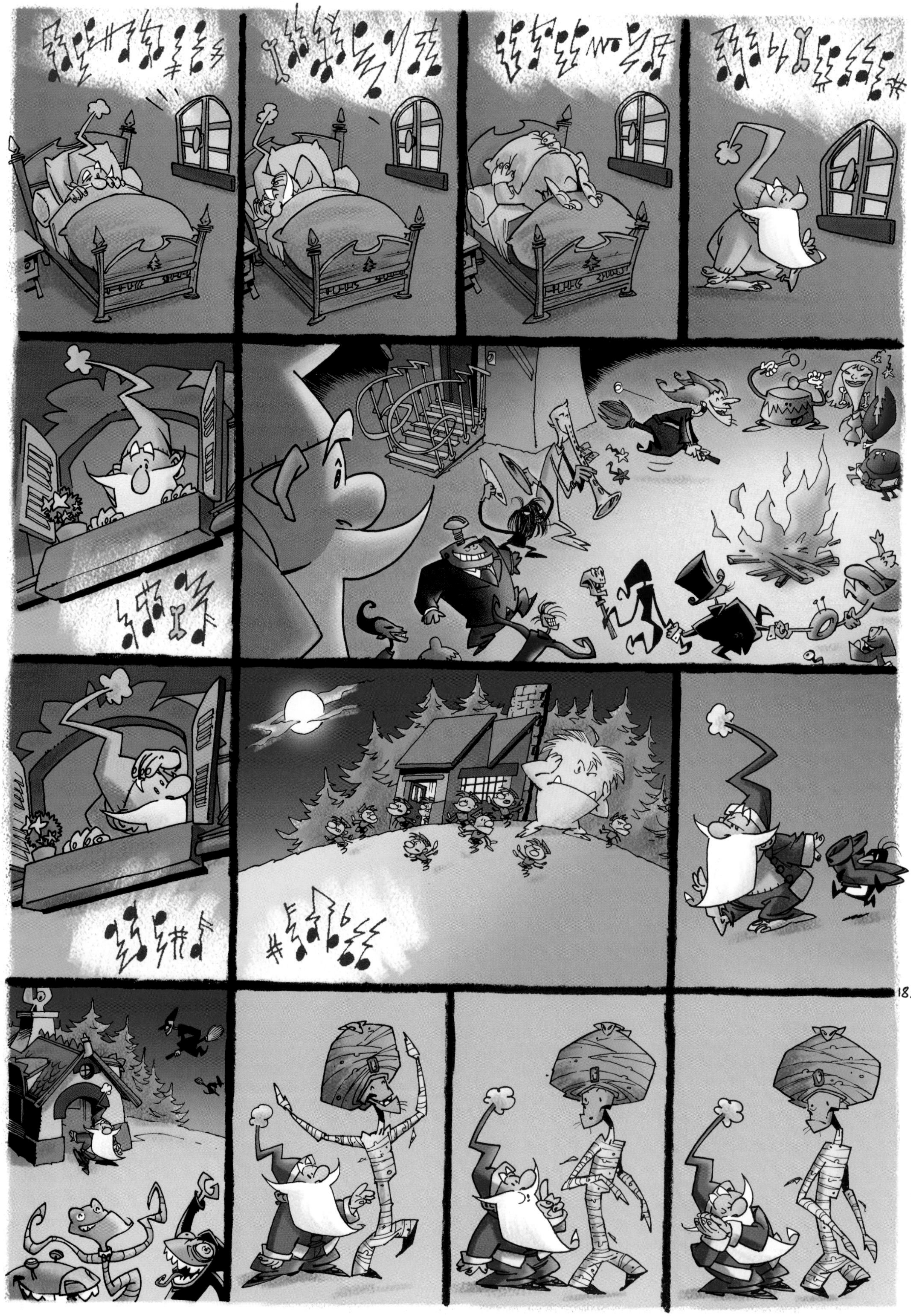

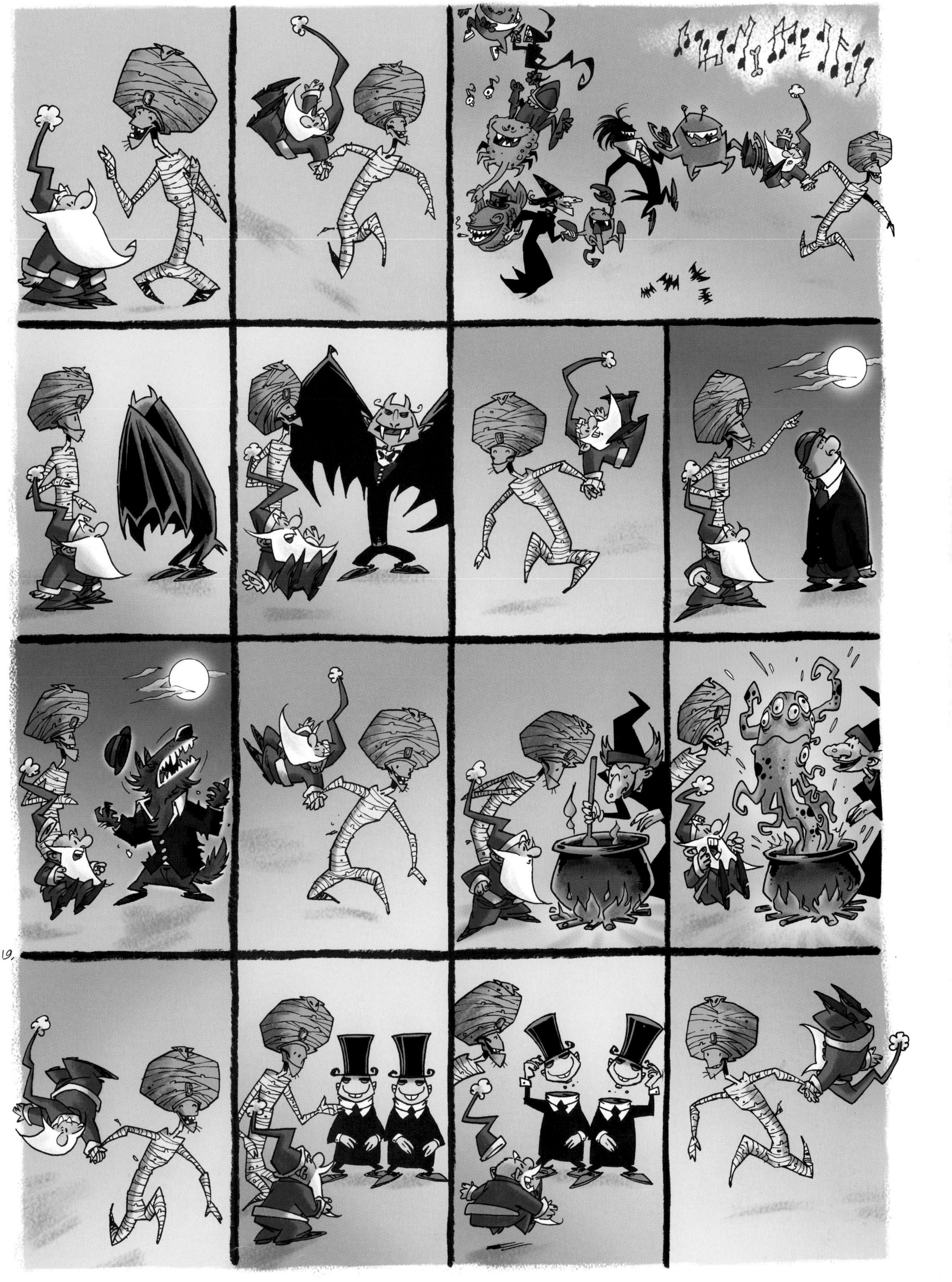

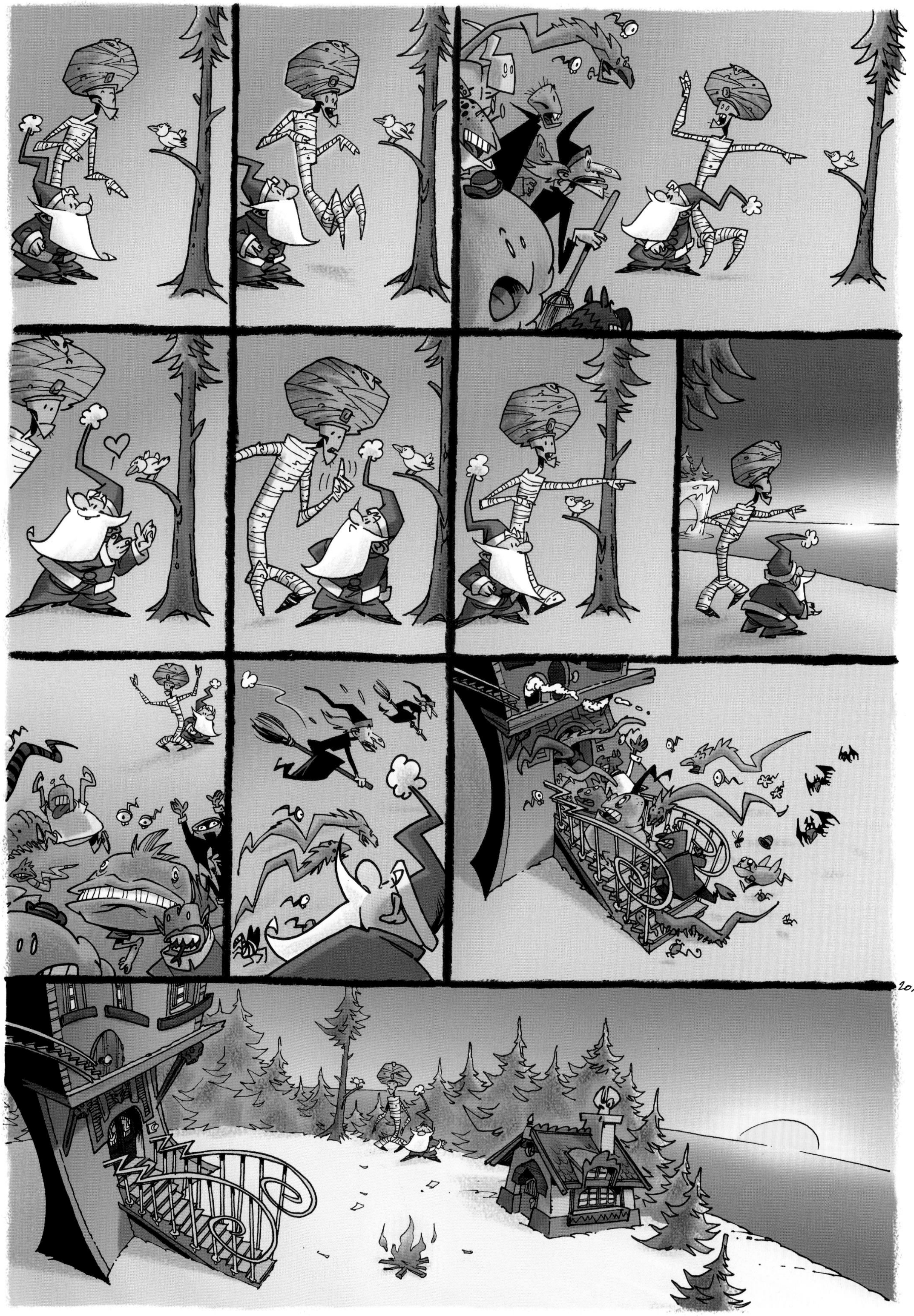

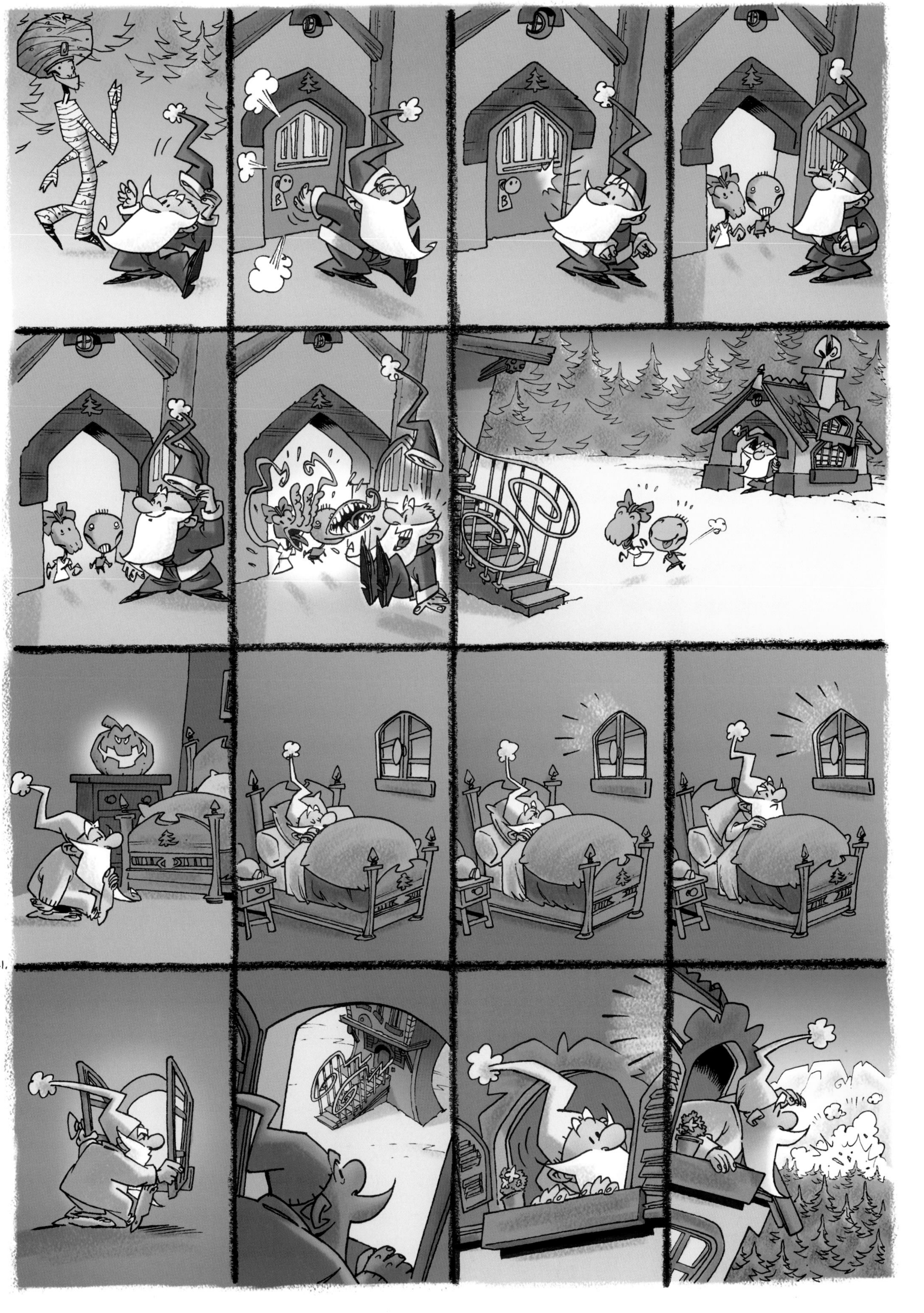
B
GY!

21.

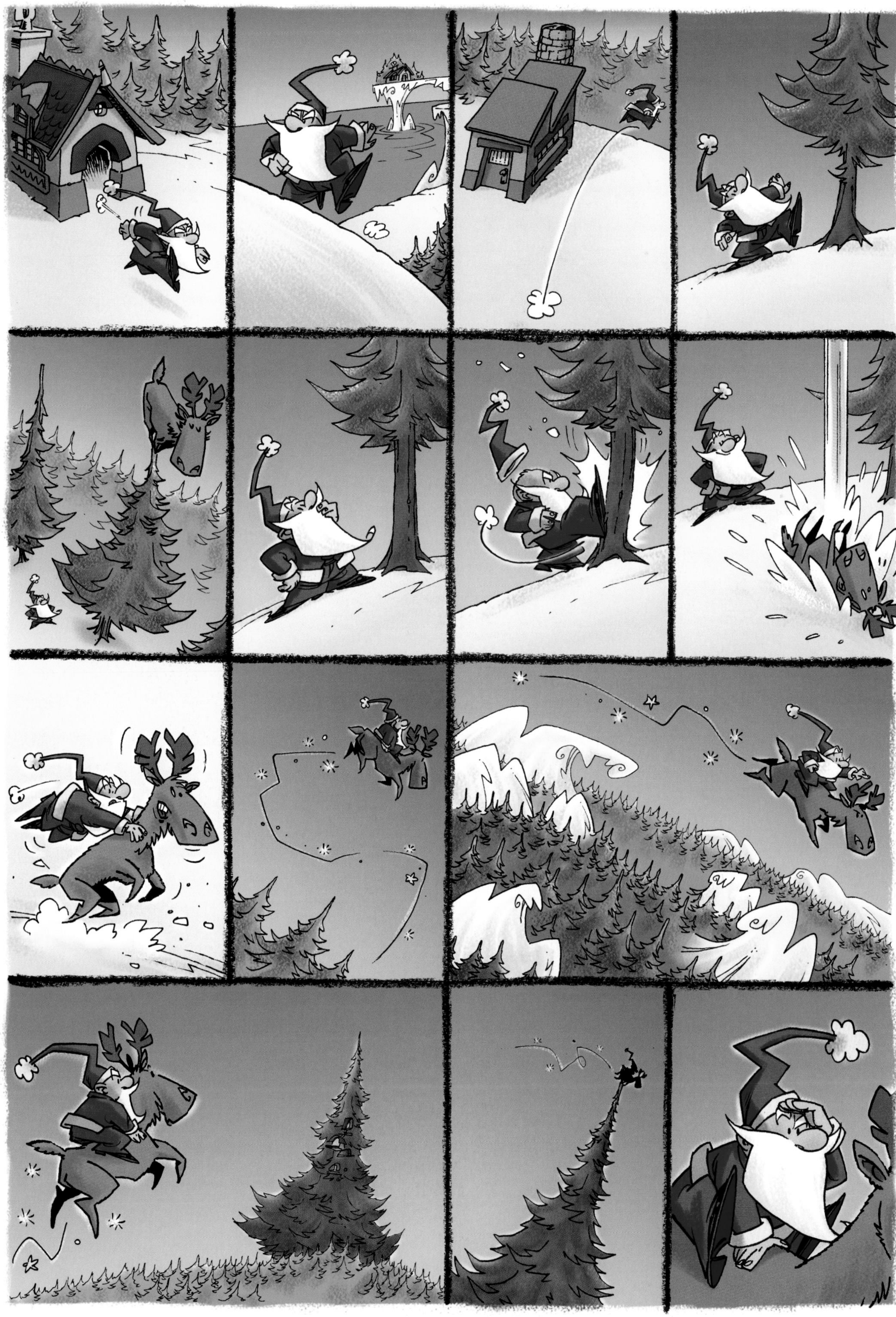

23,

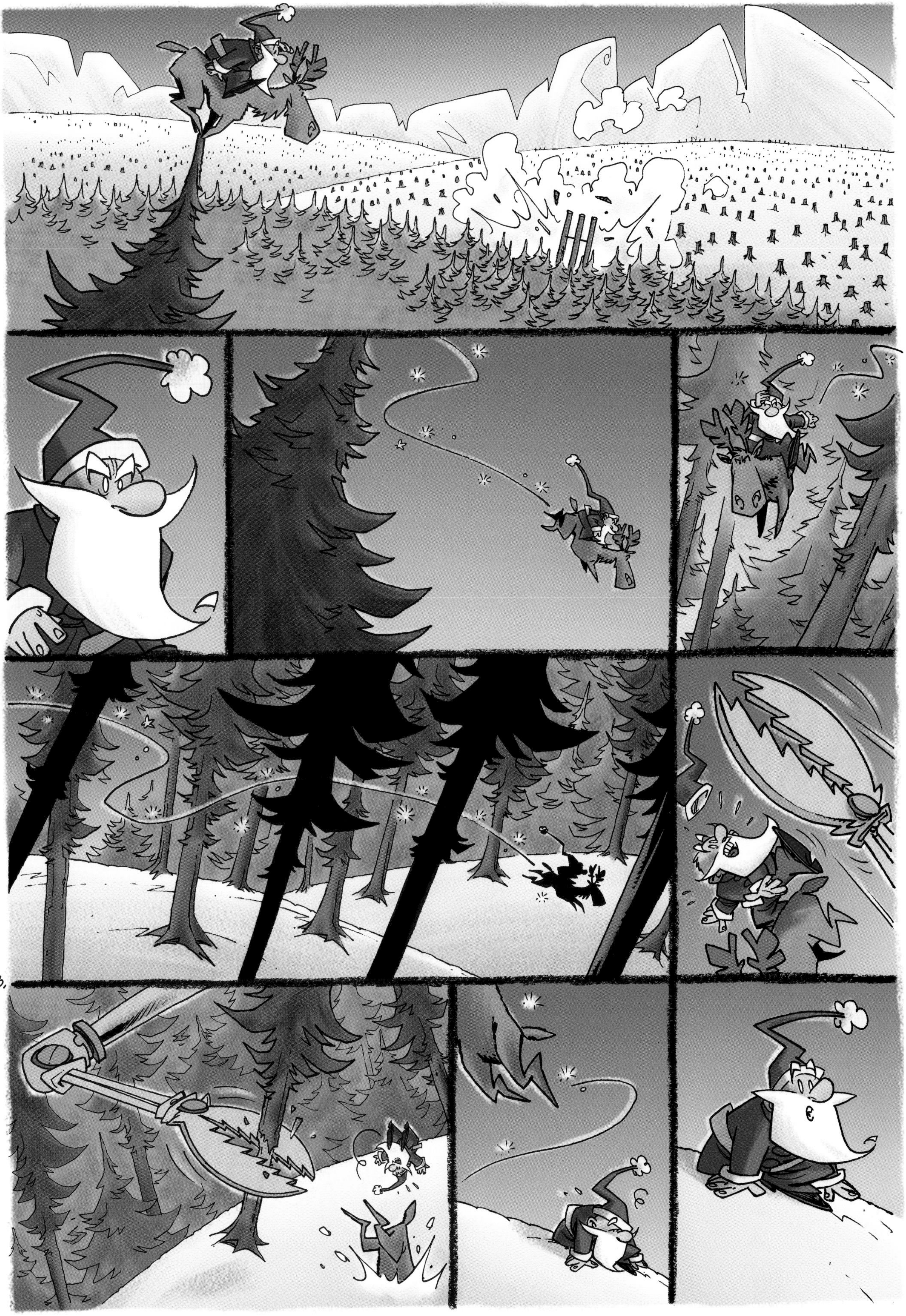

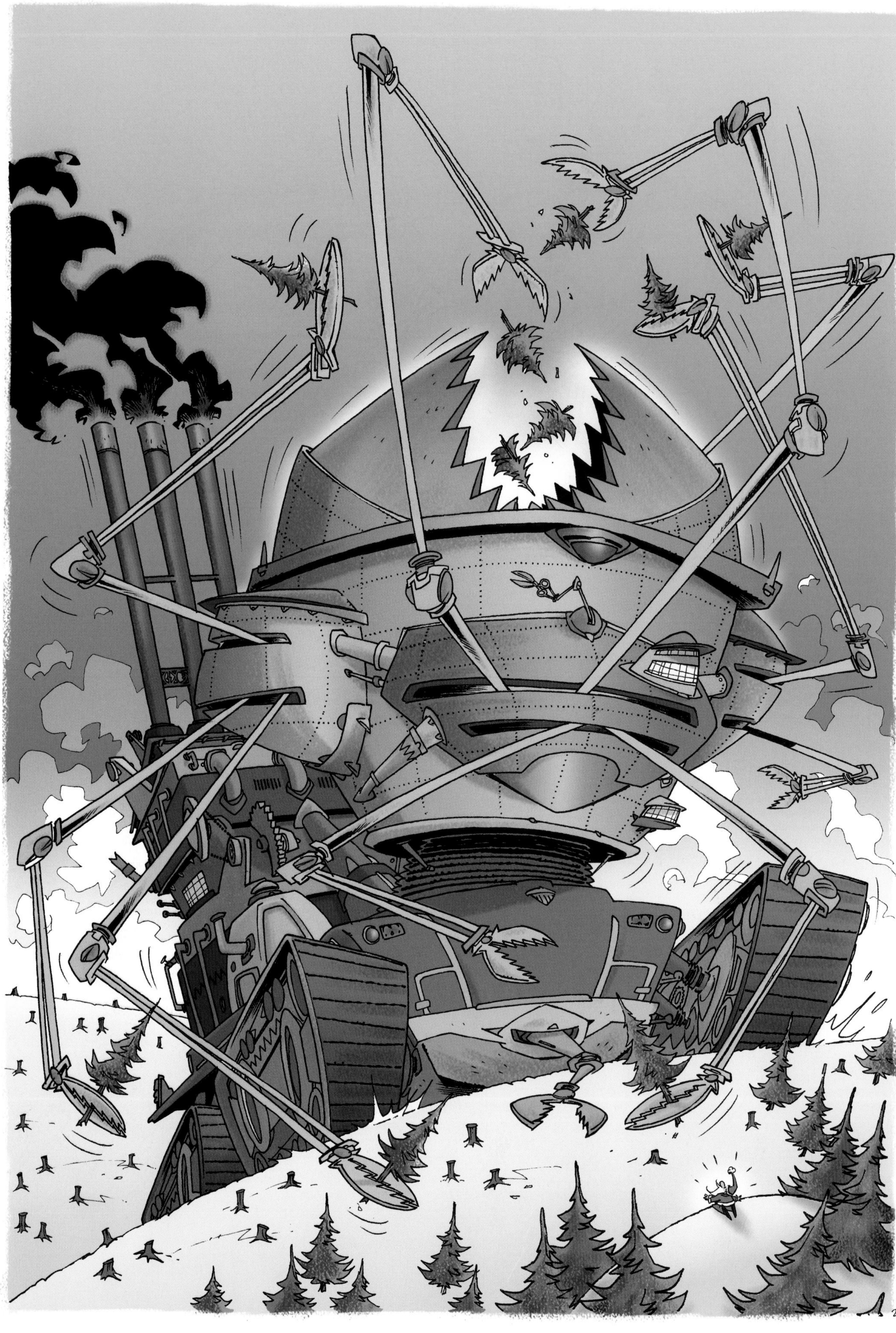

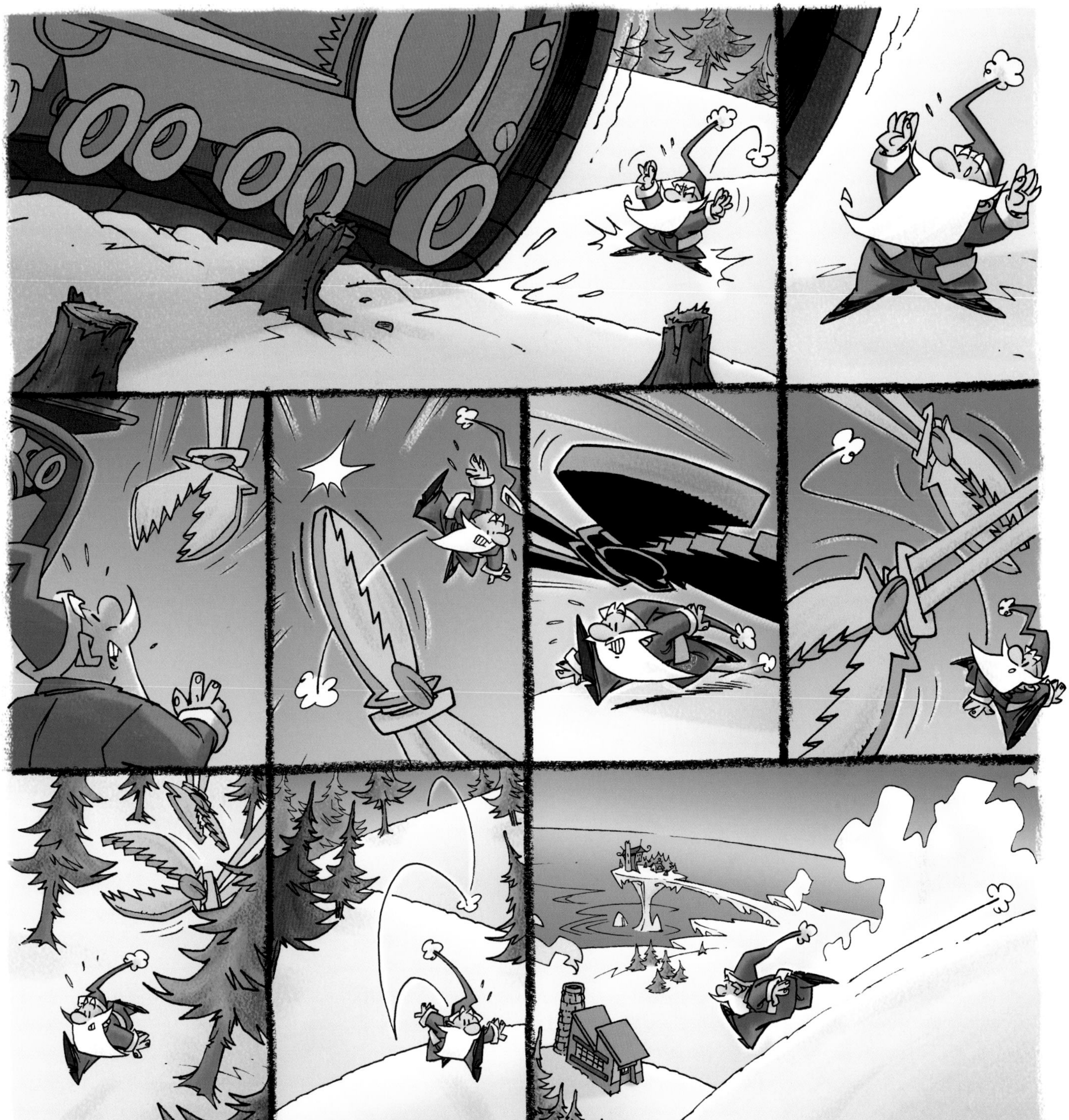

25.

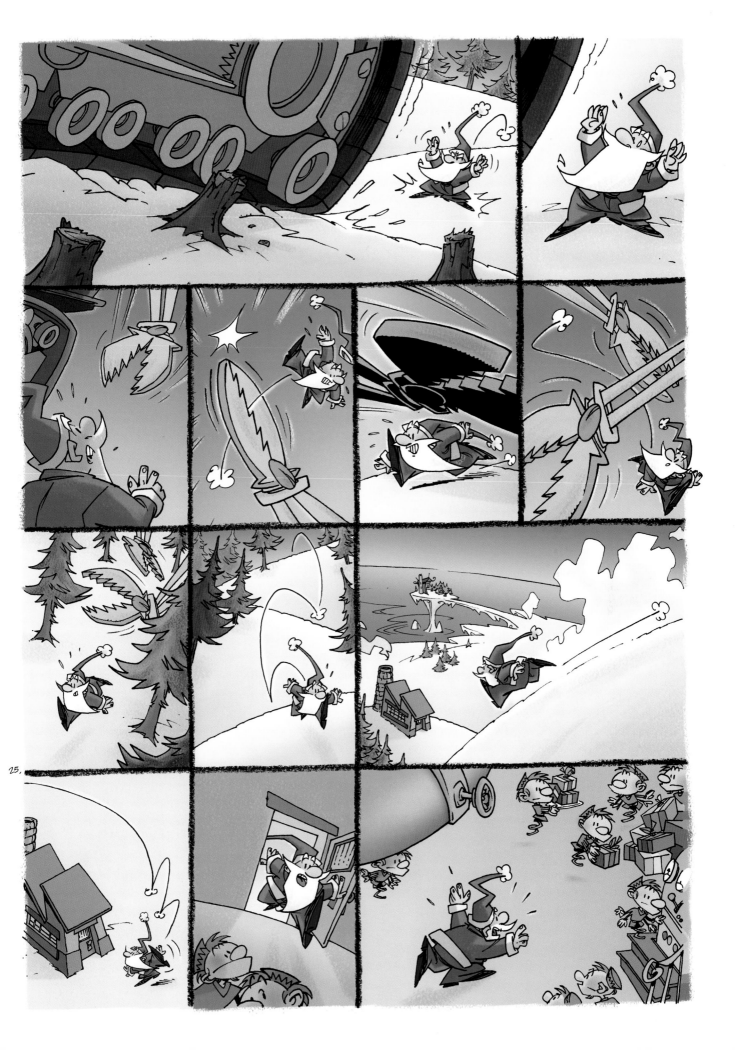

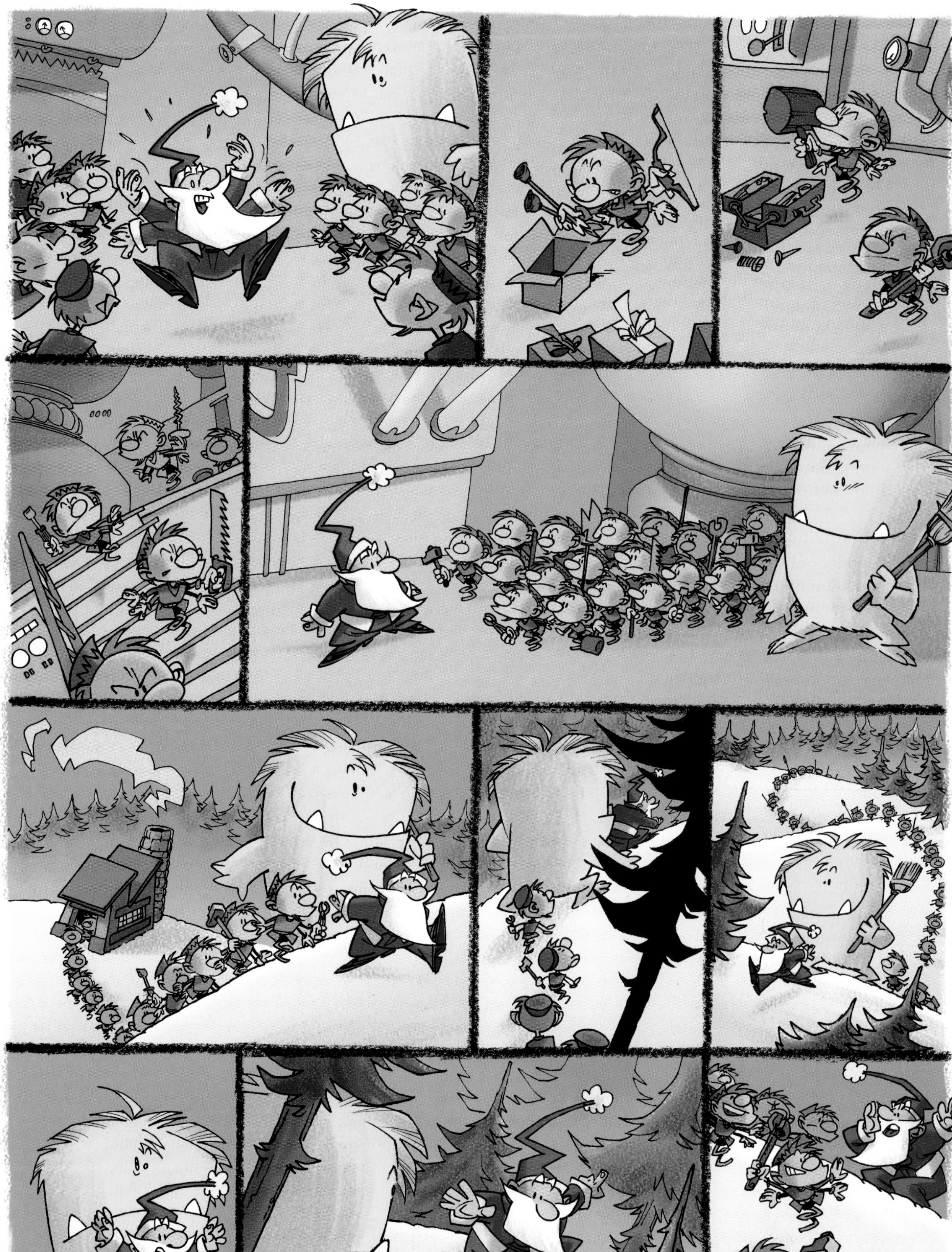

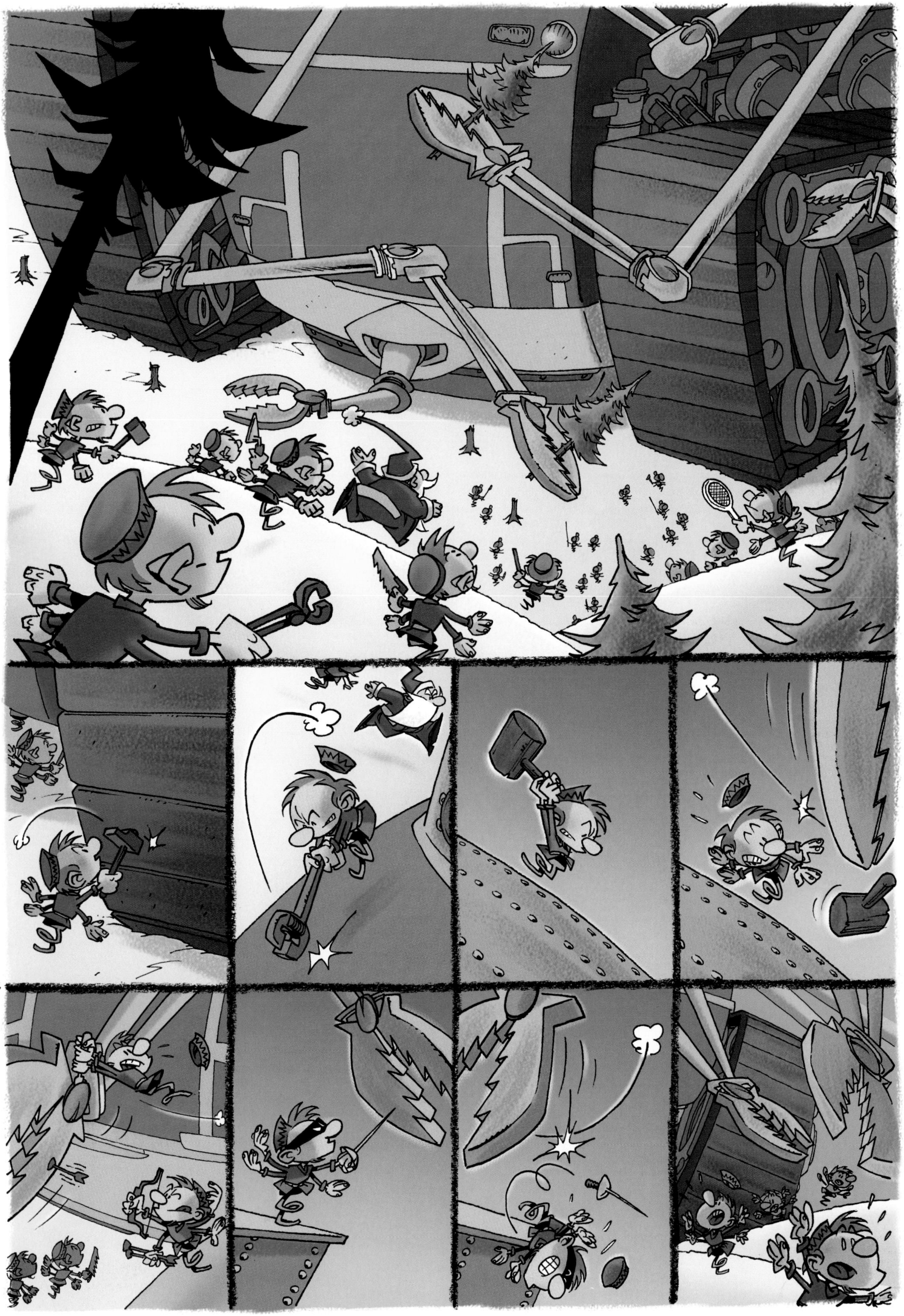

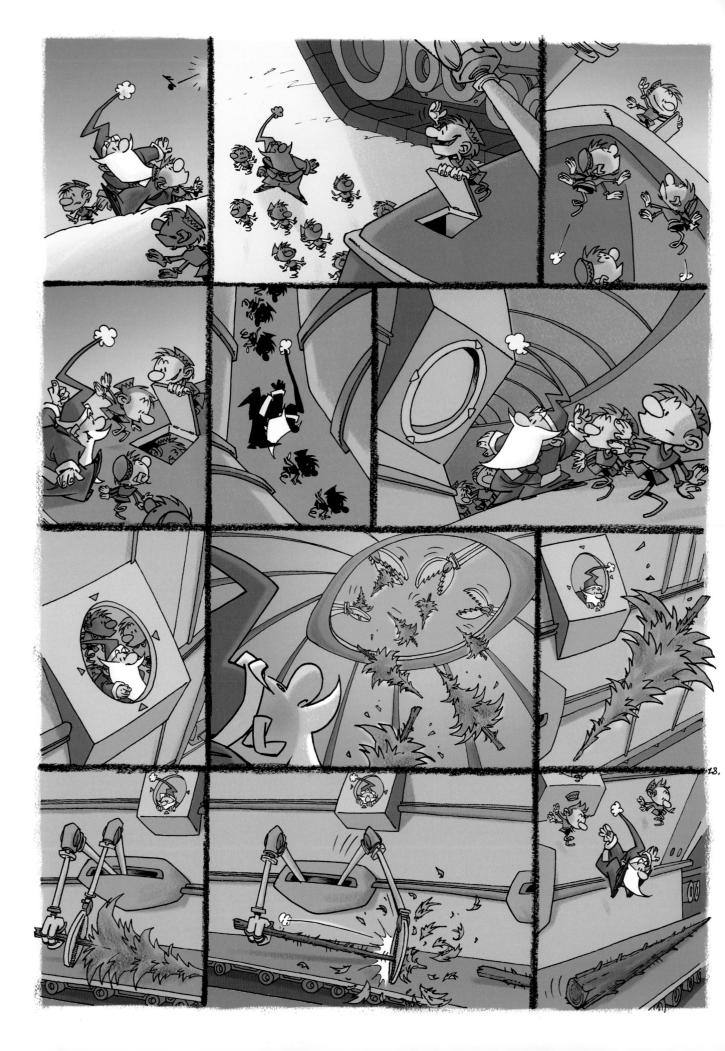

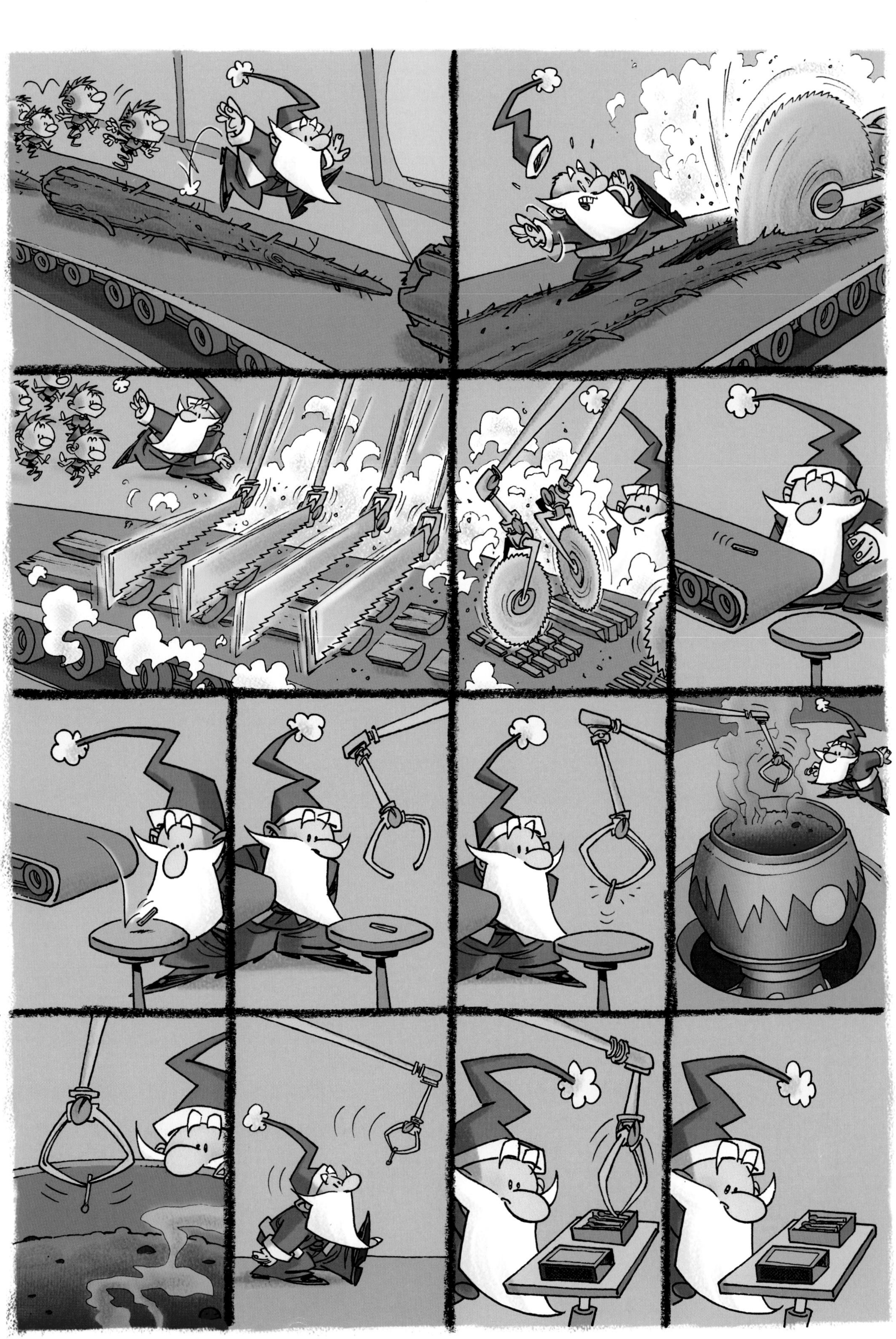

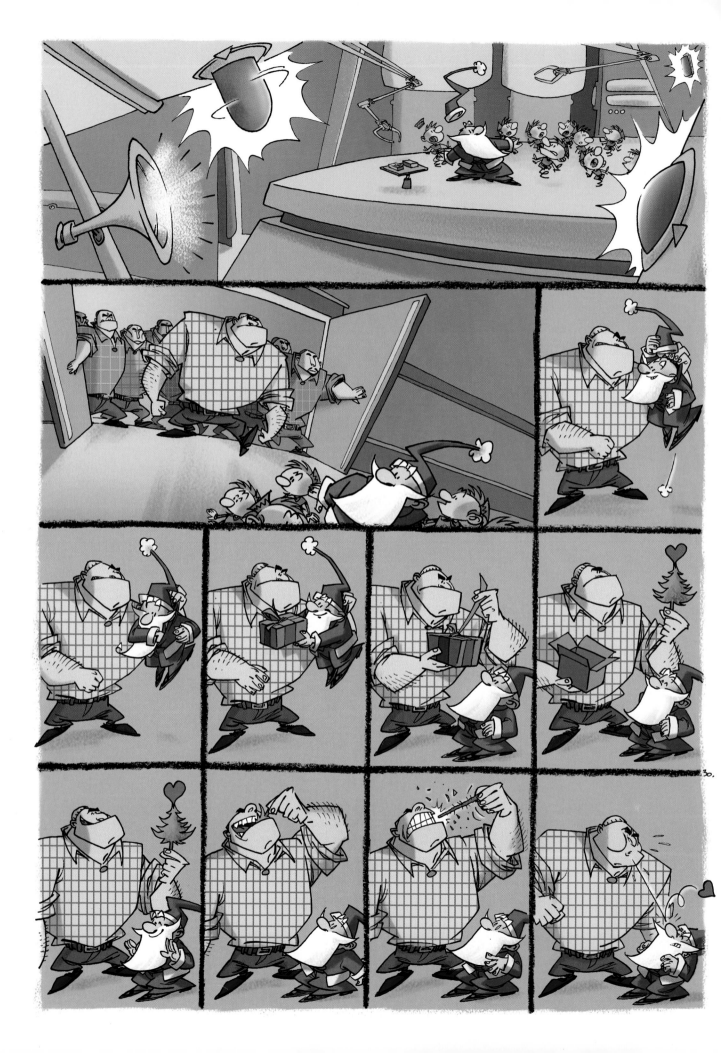

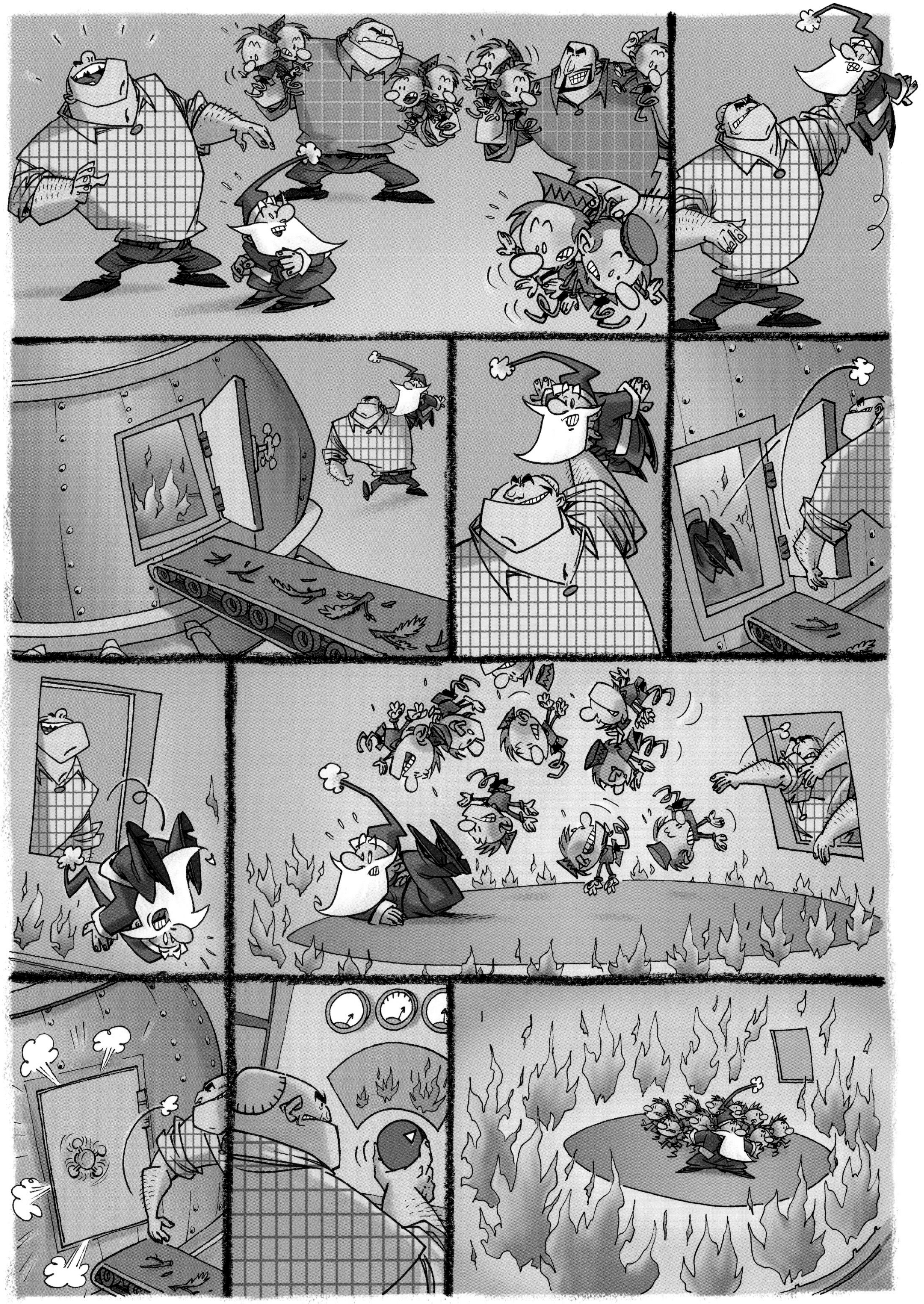

31.

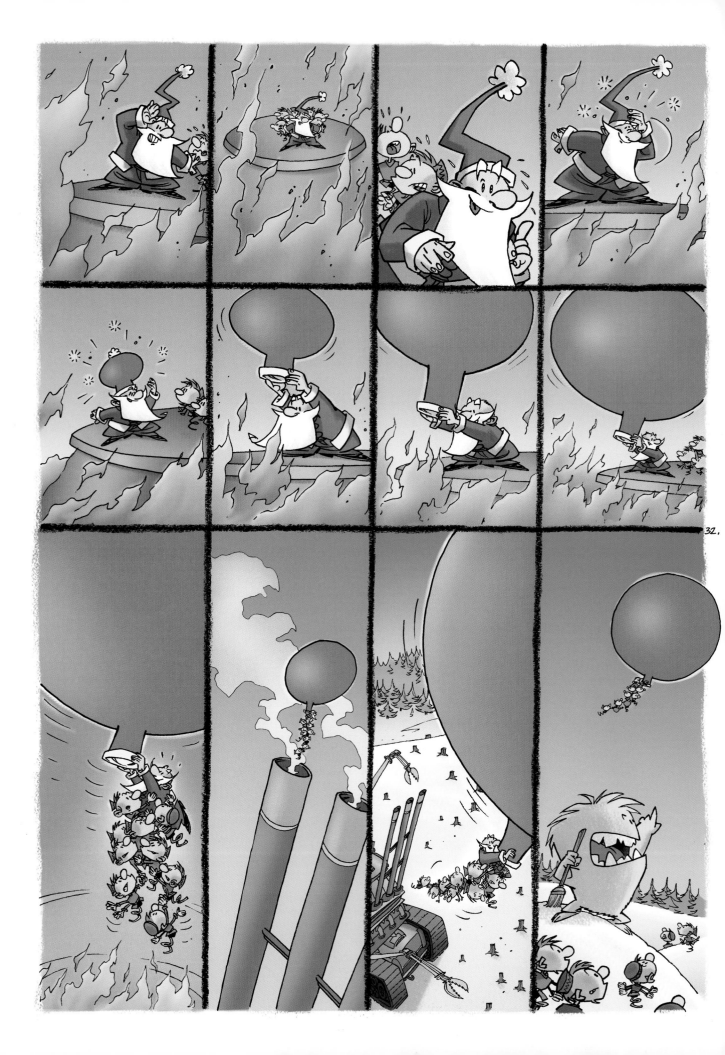

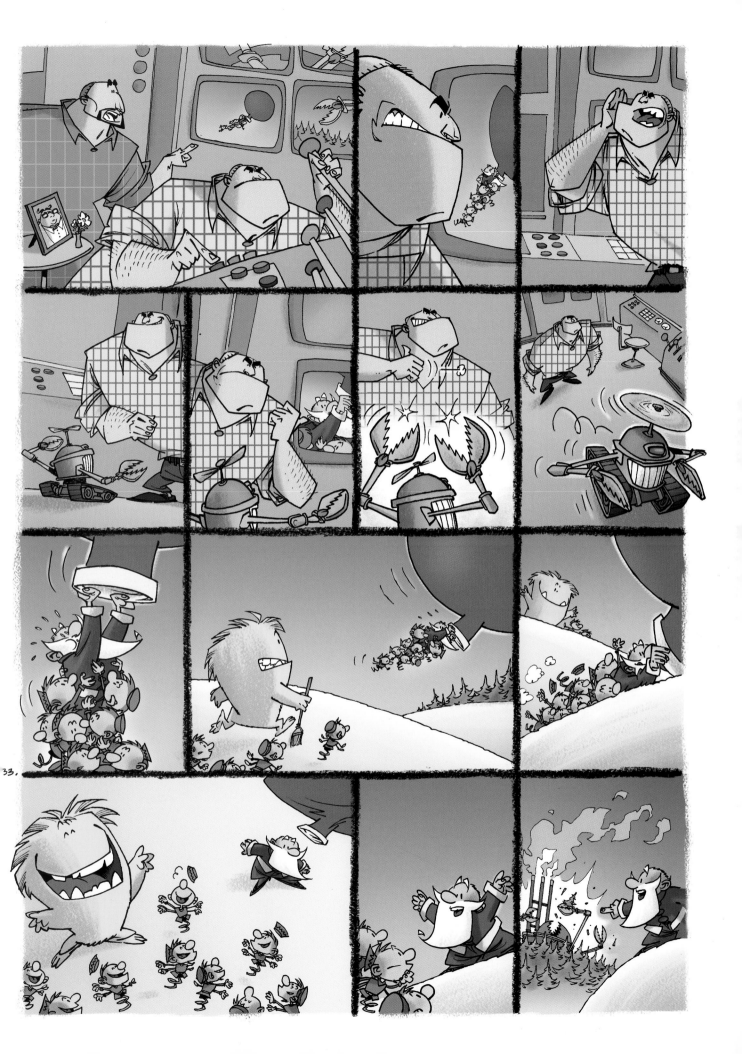

33.

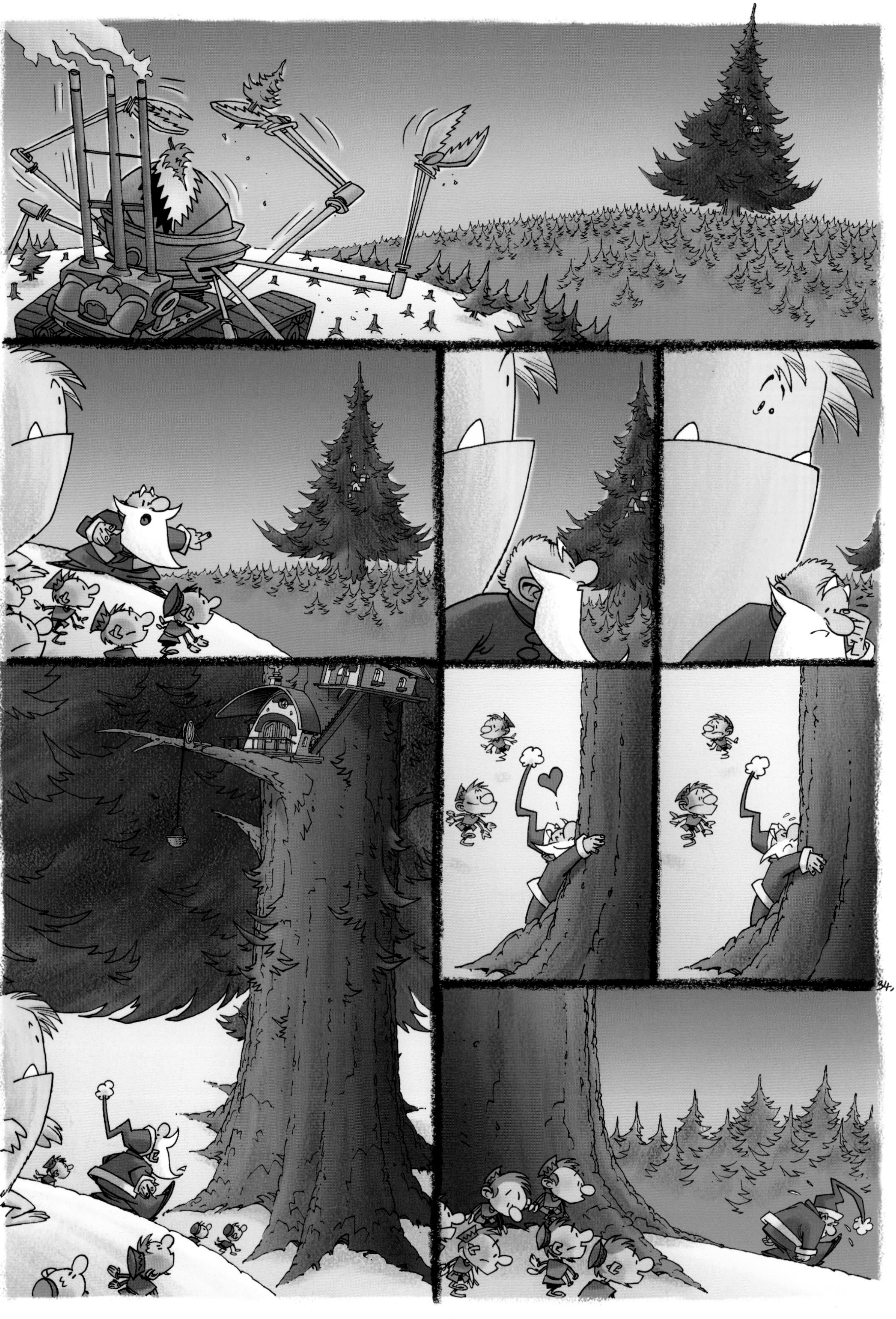

34.

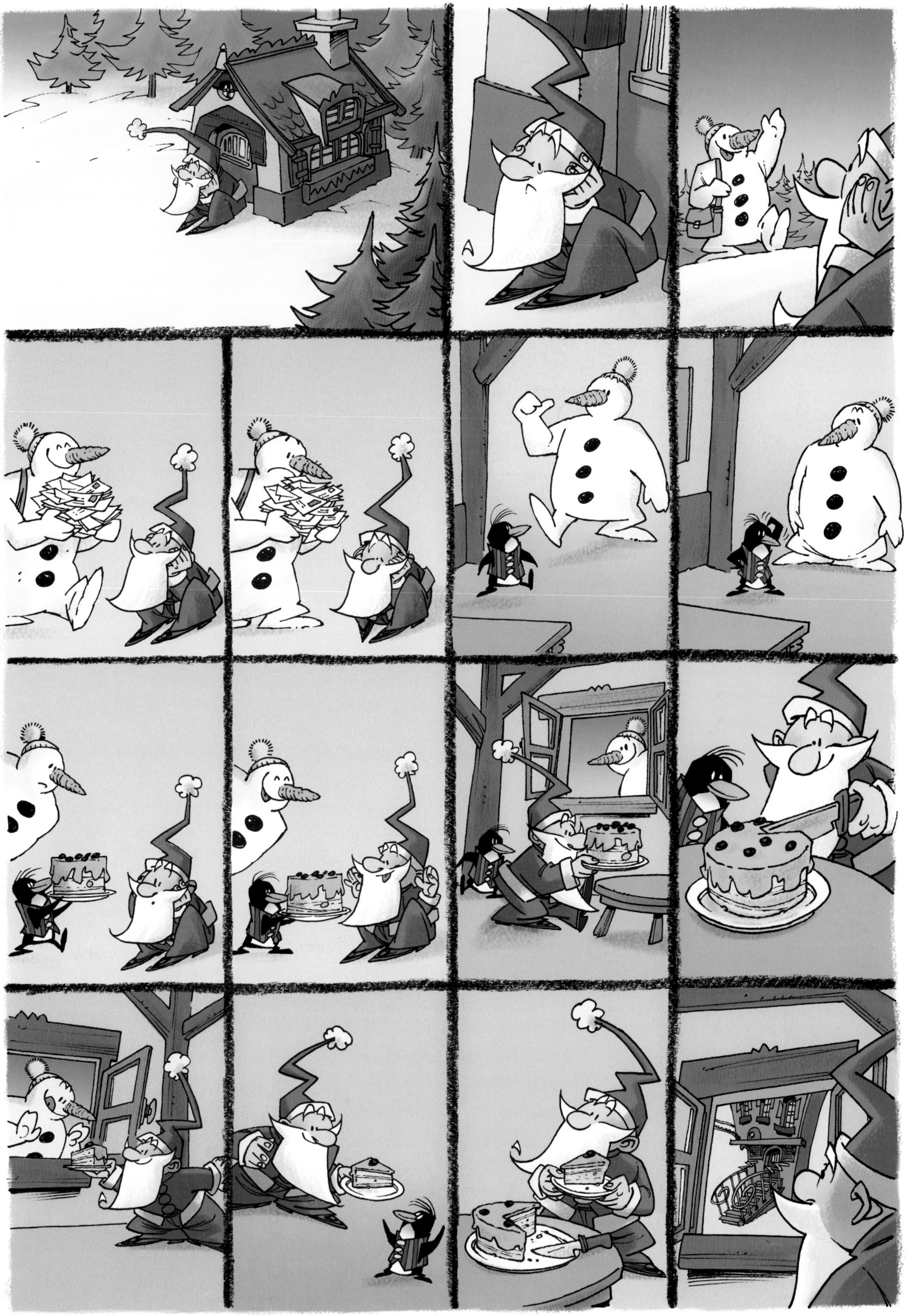

35.

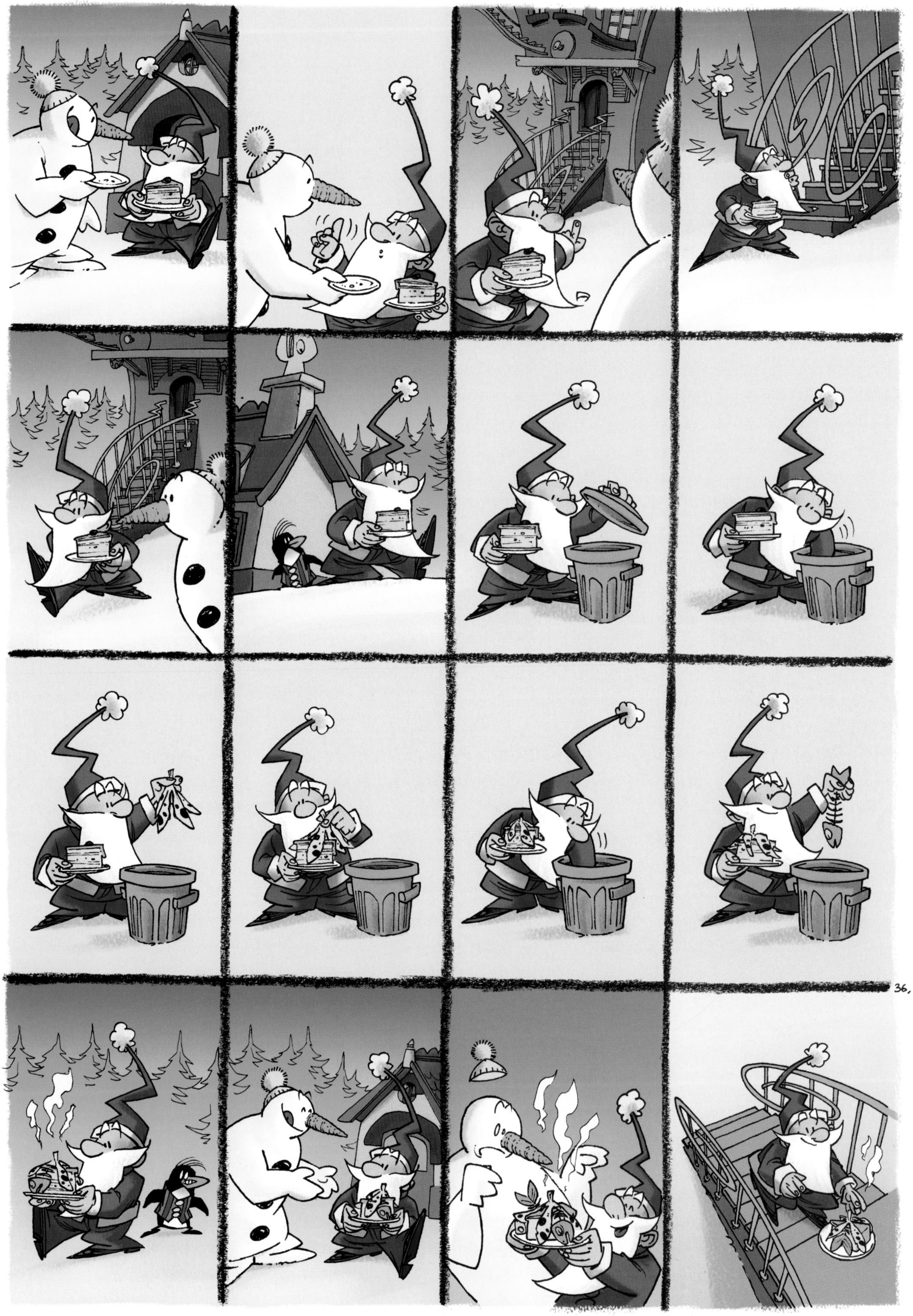

36,

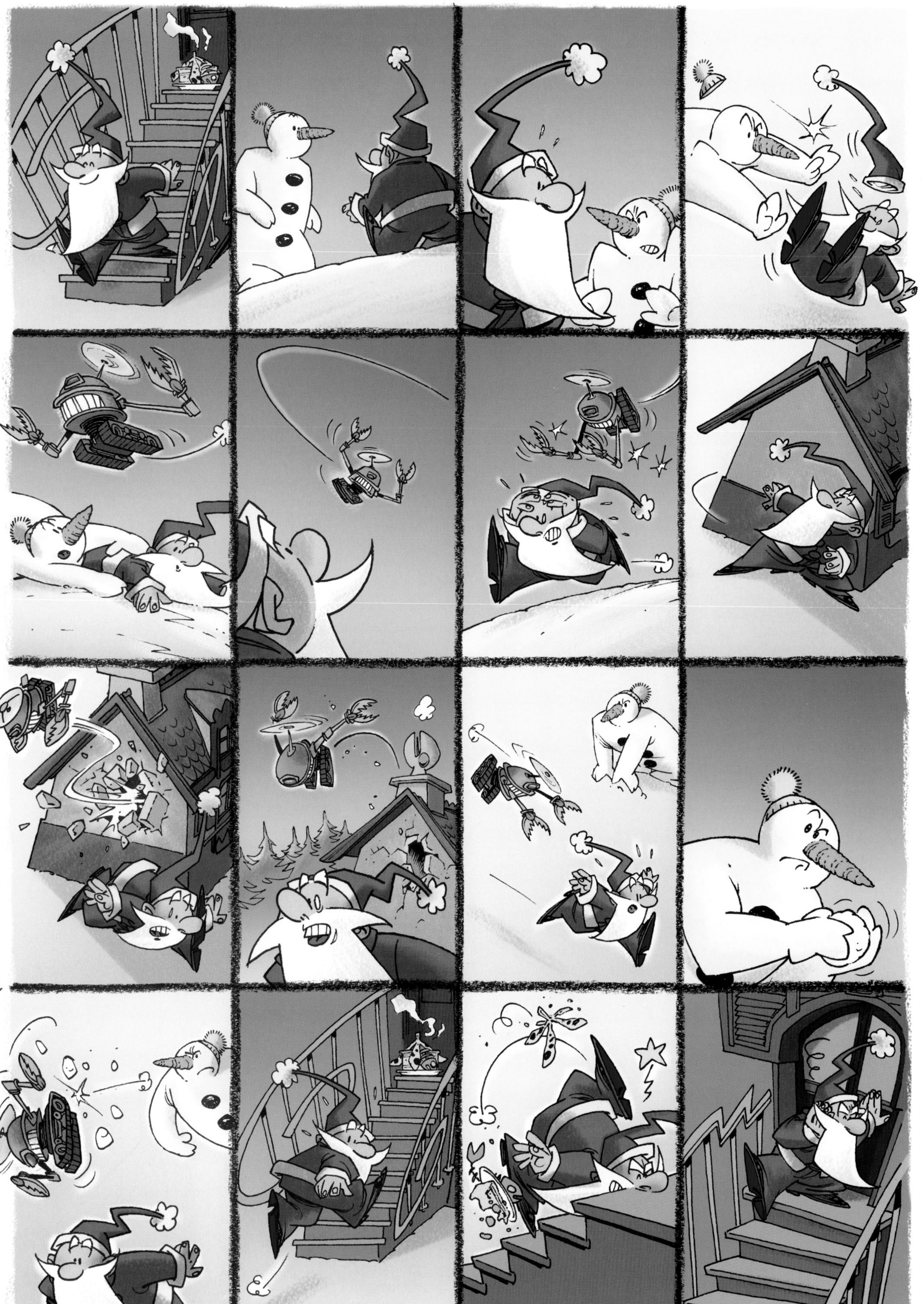

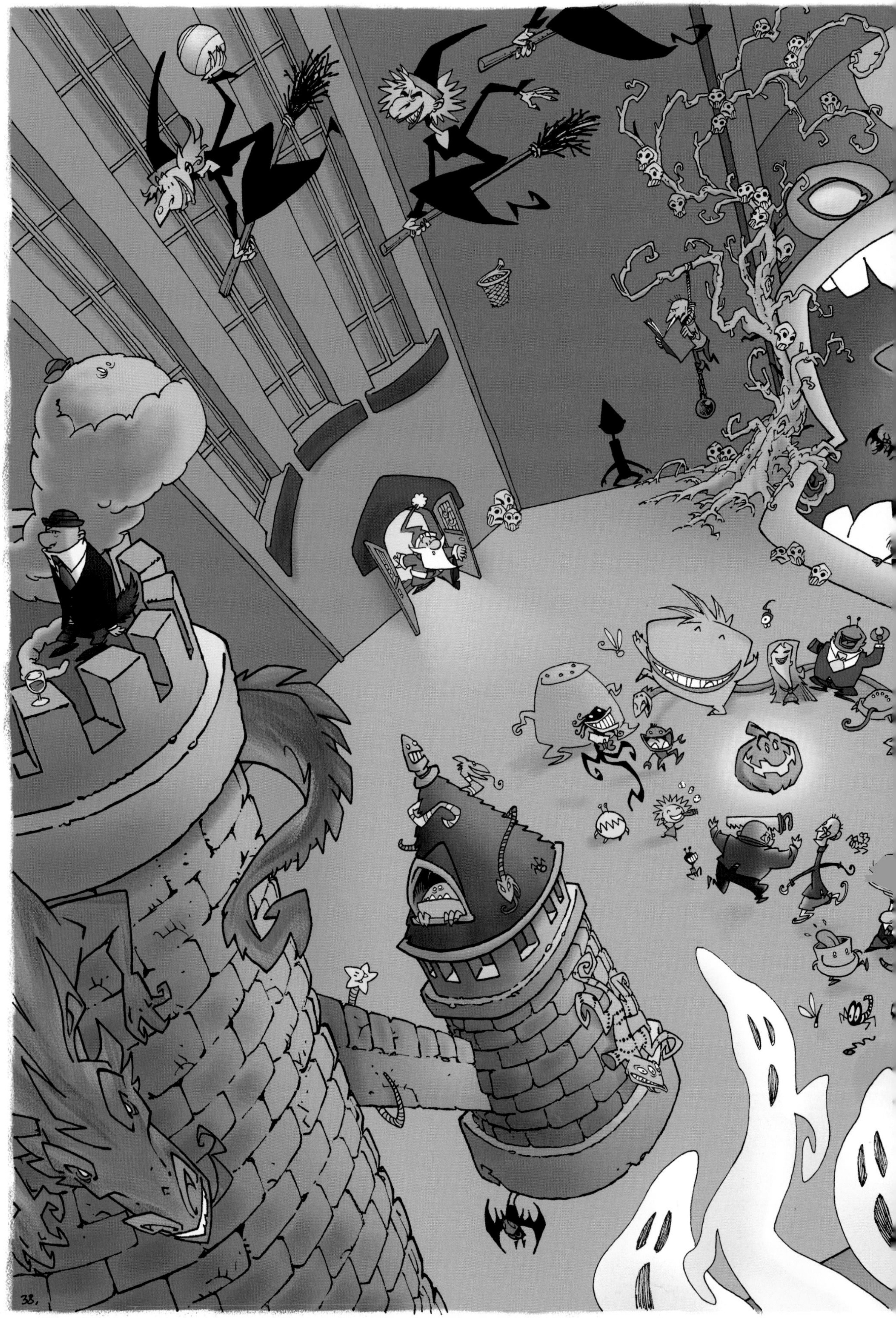

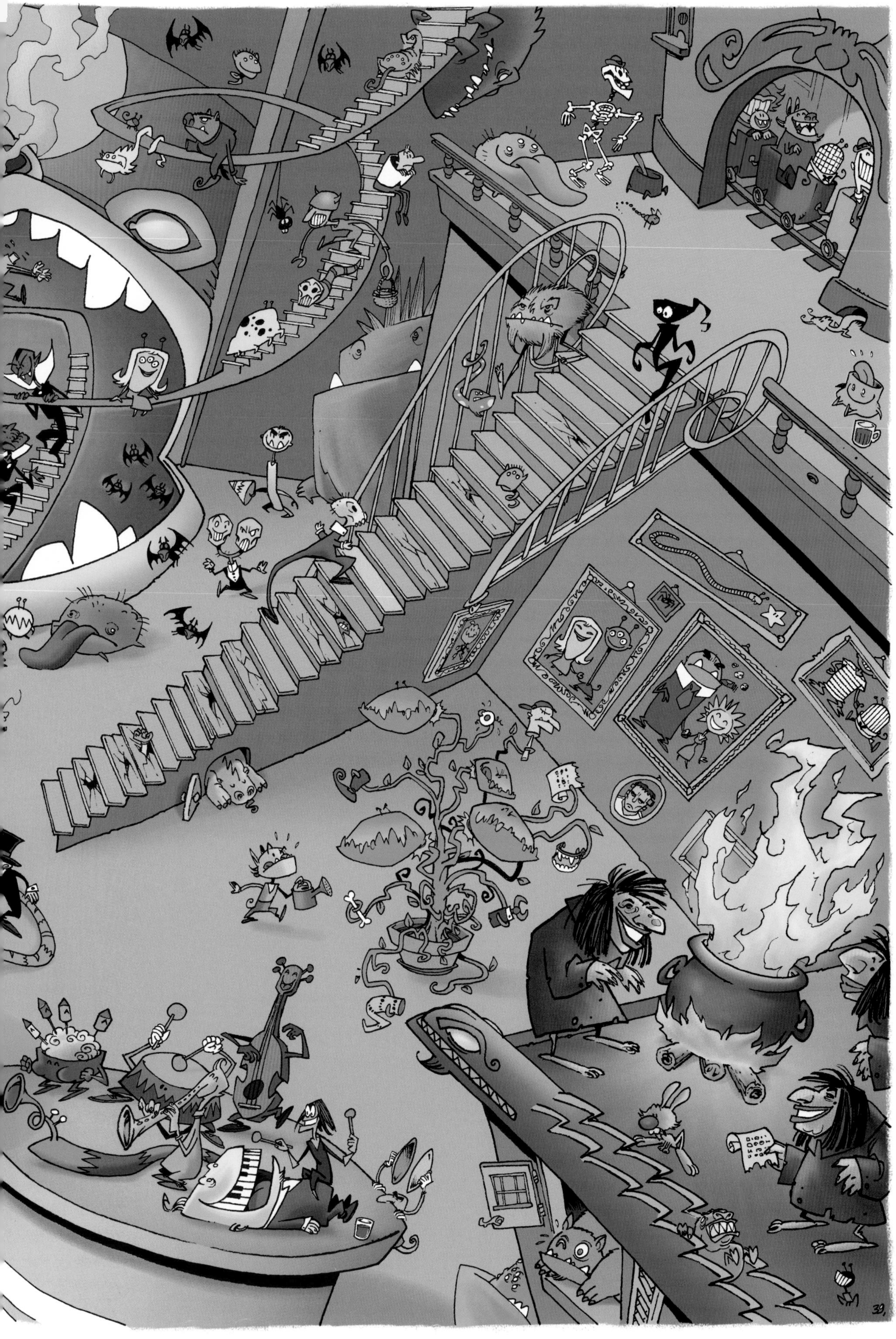

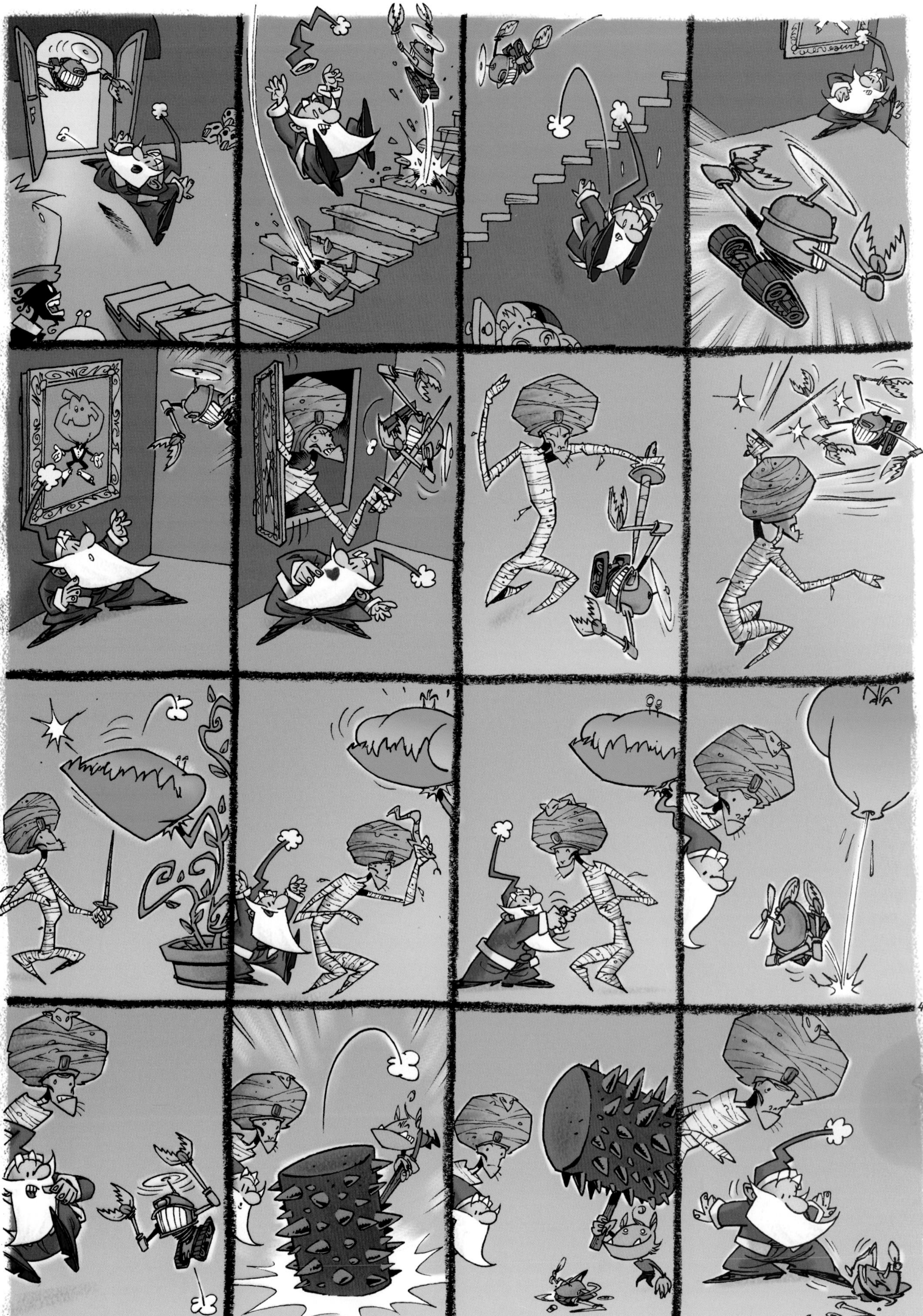

40

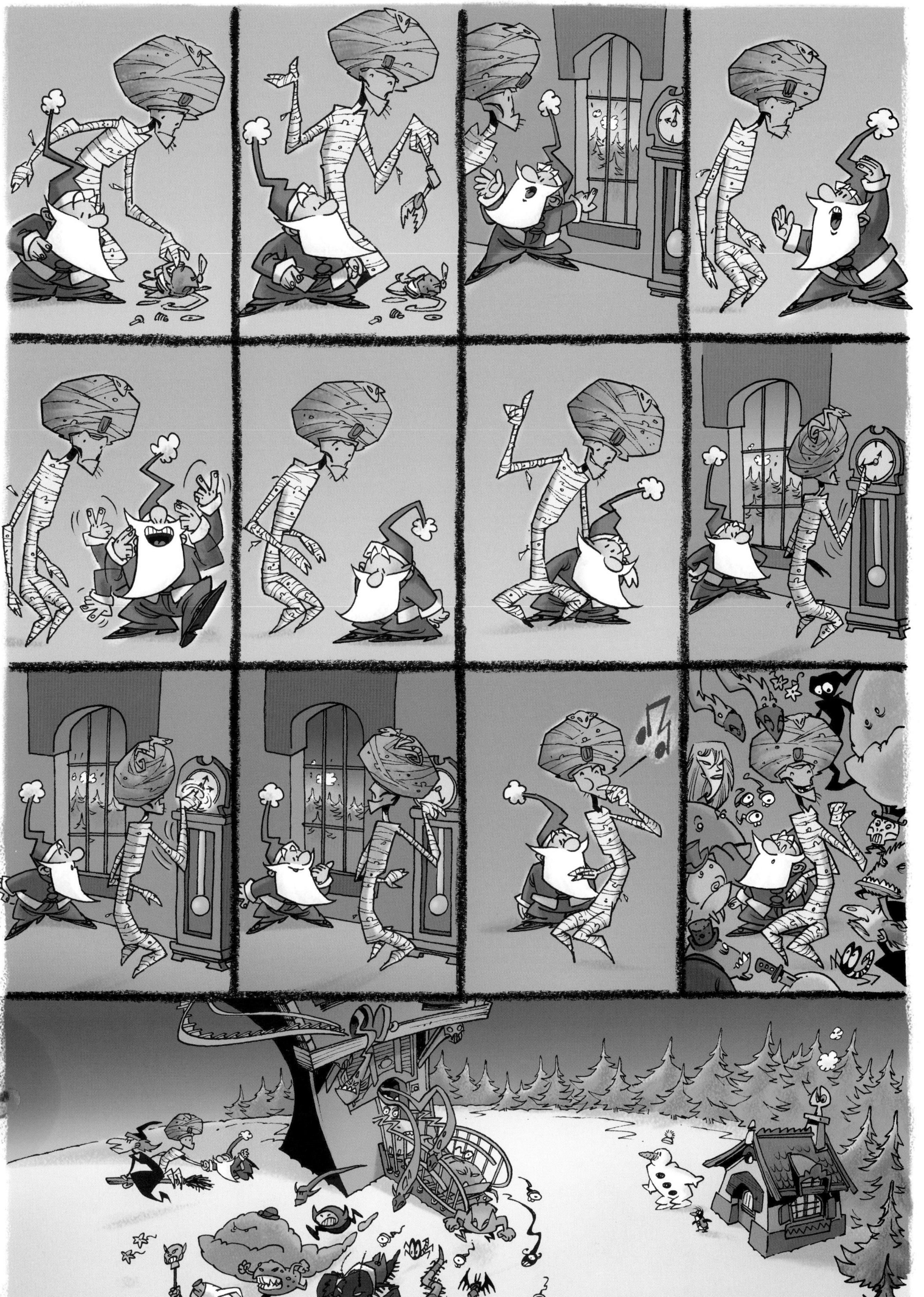

41,

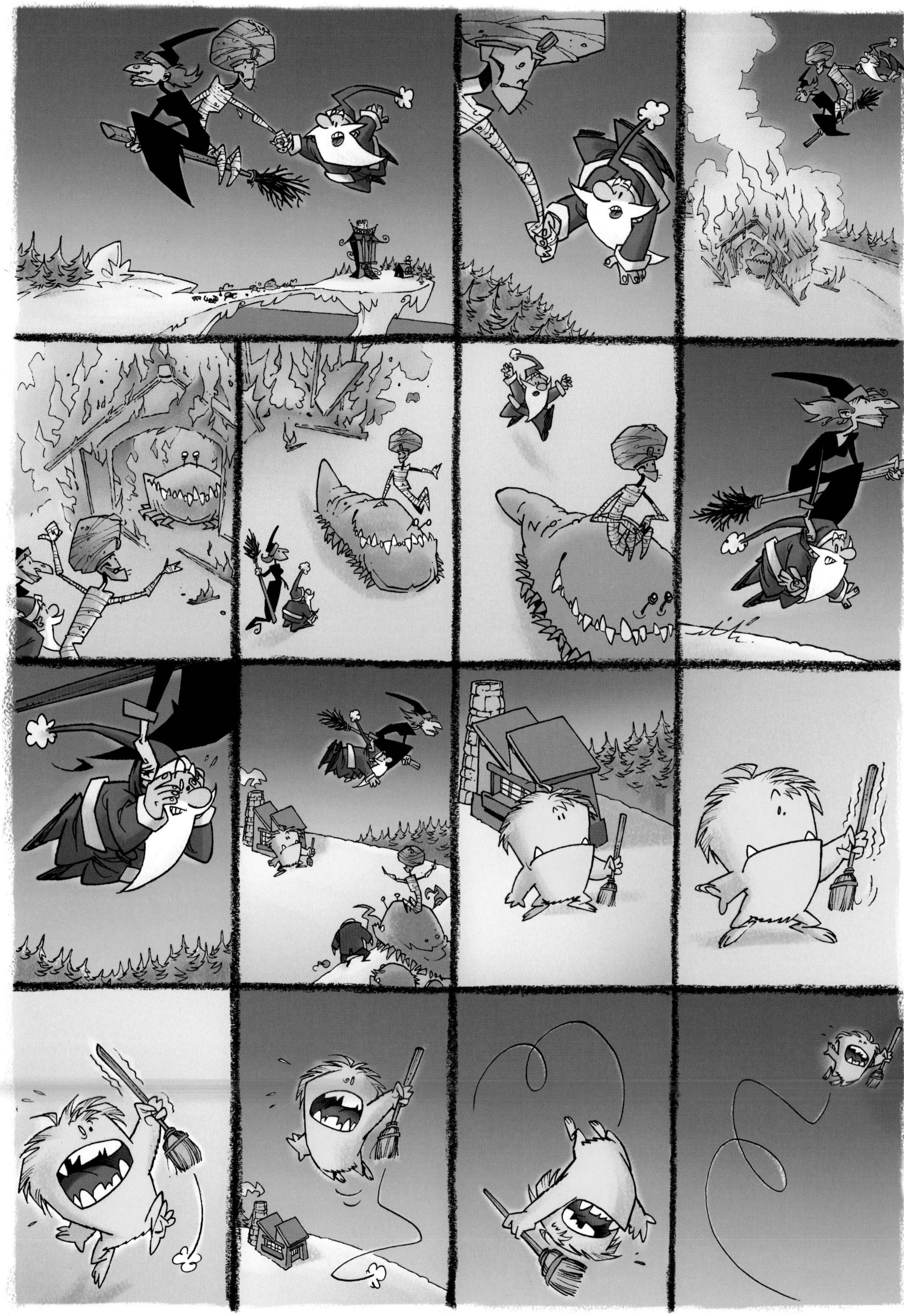

42,

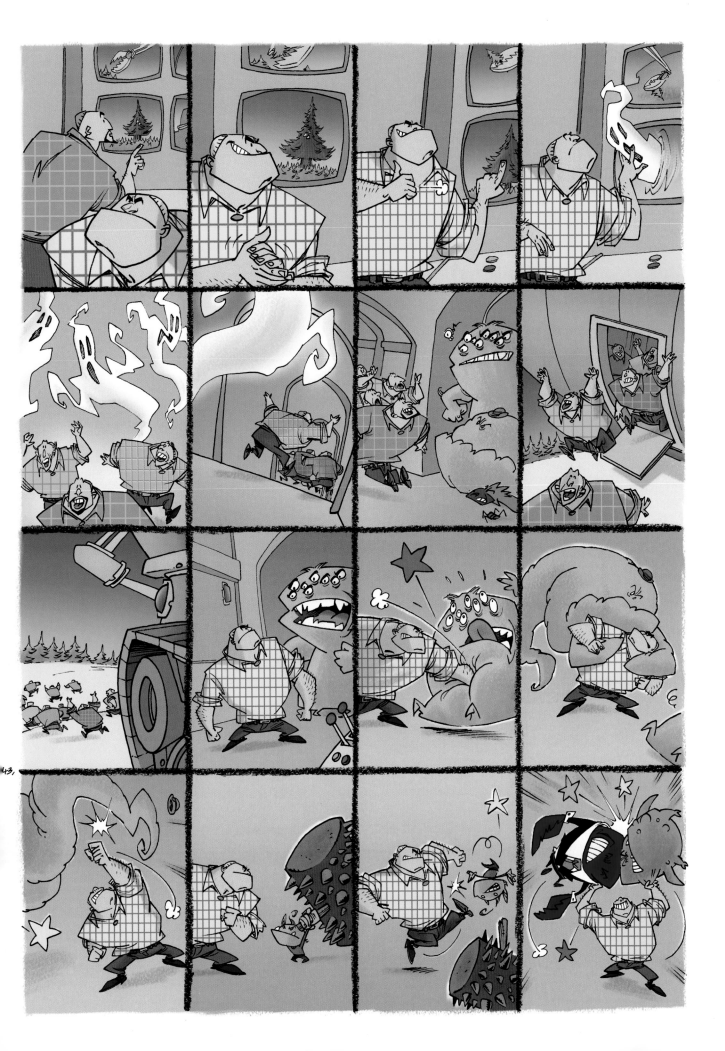

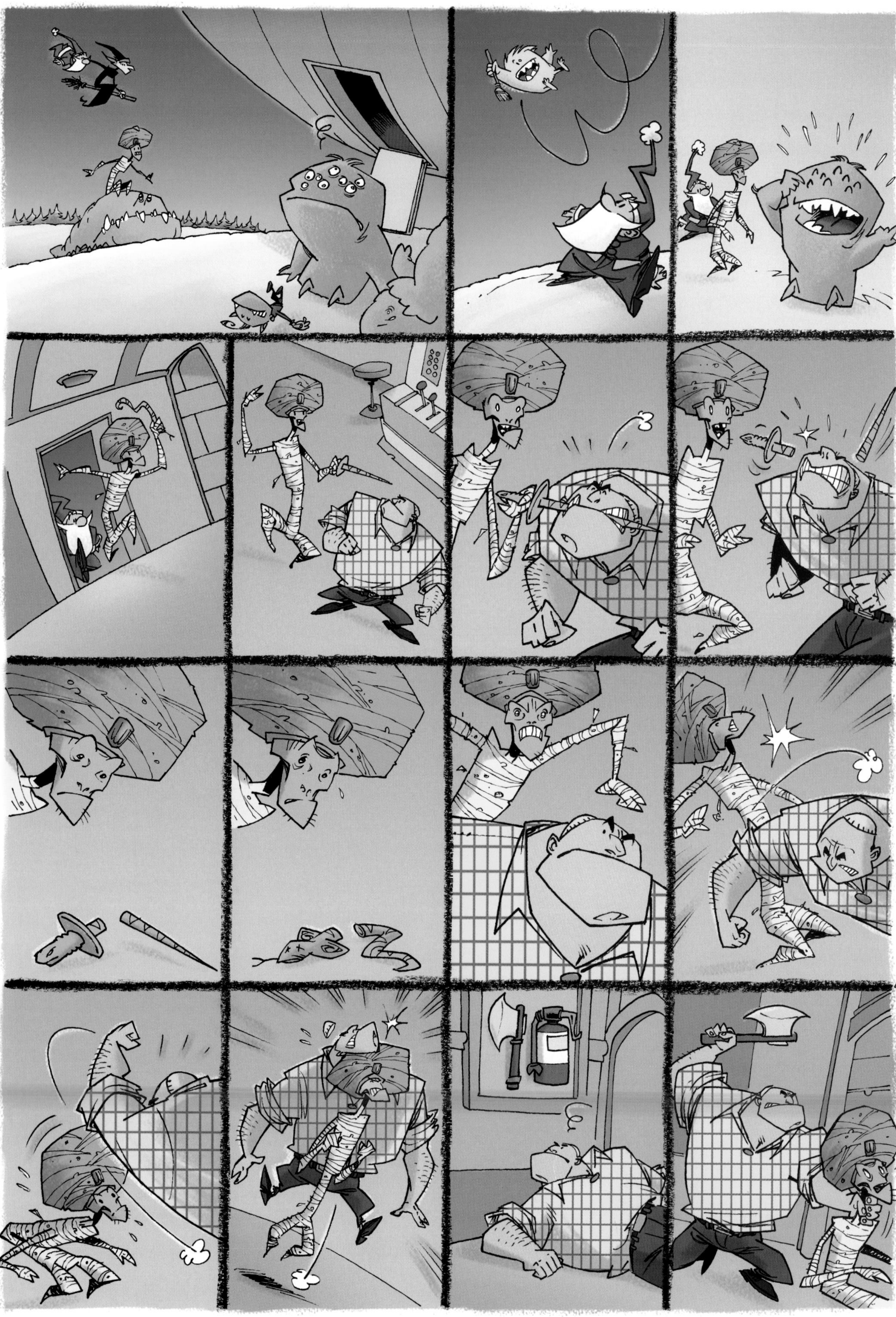

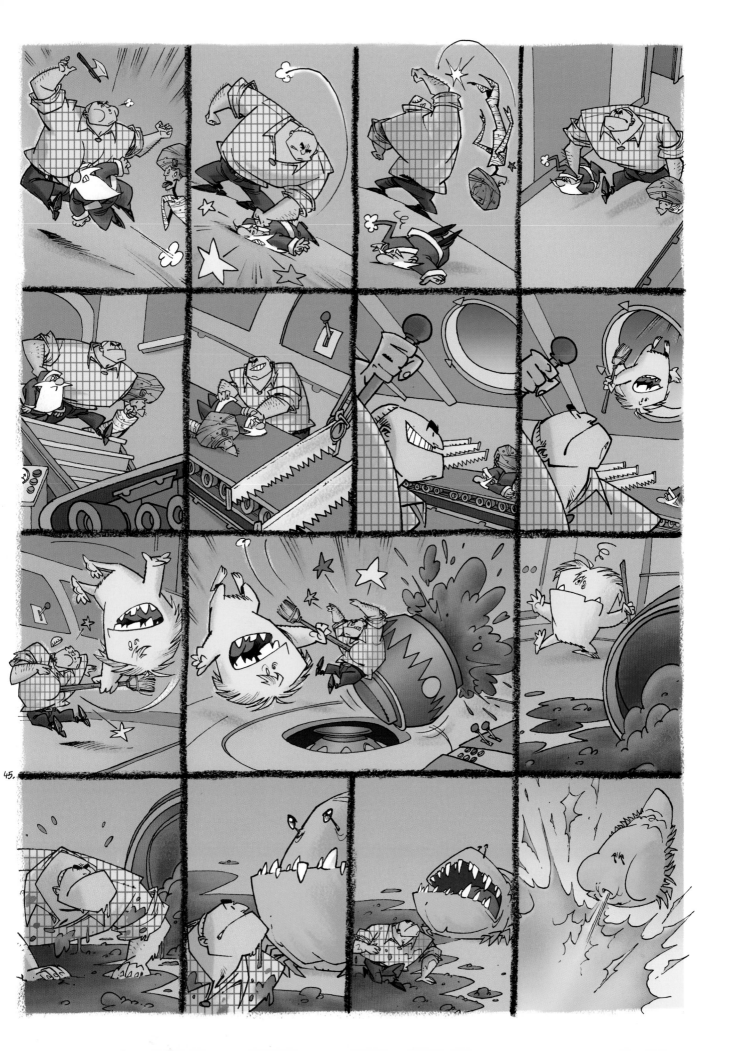

45.

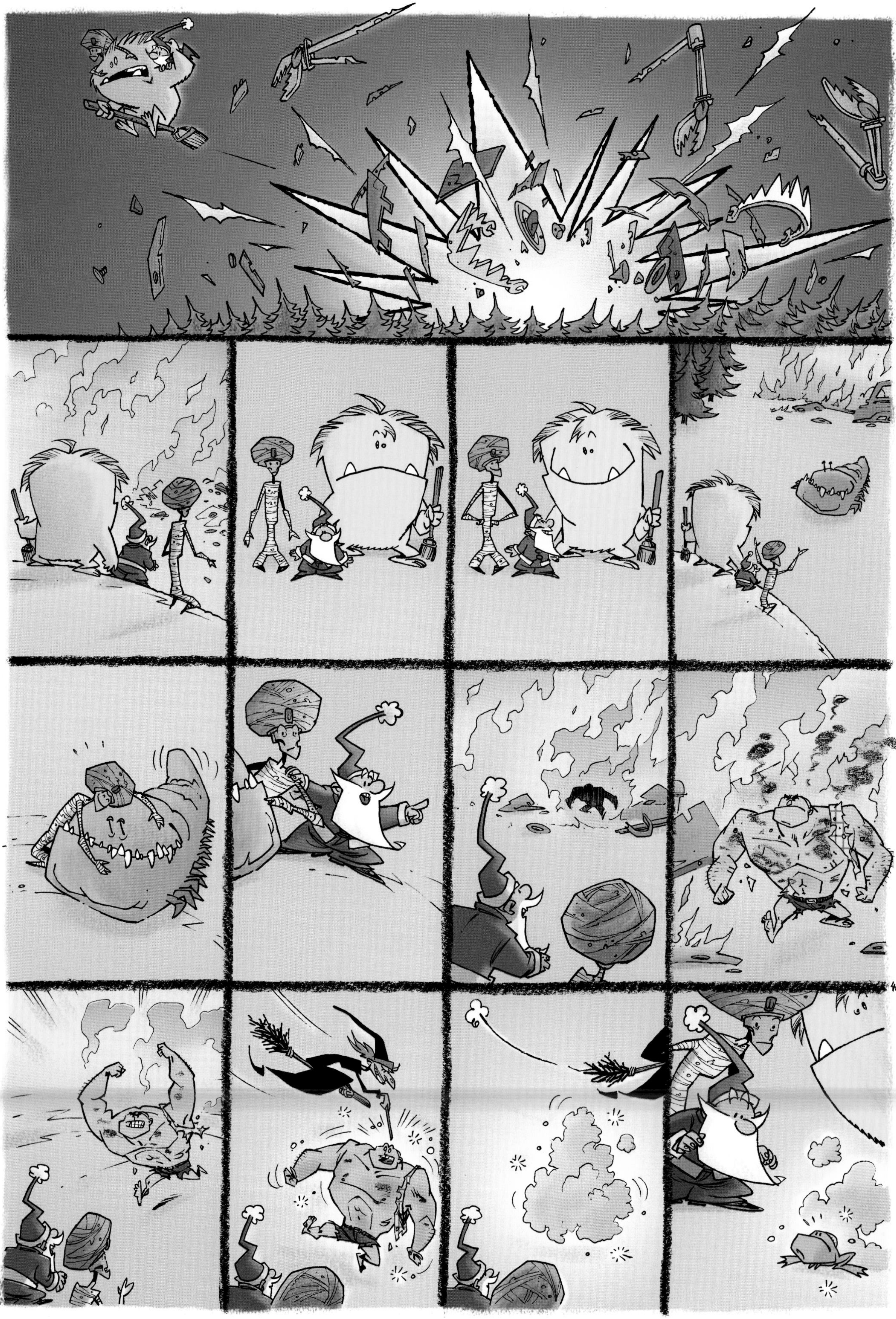

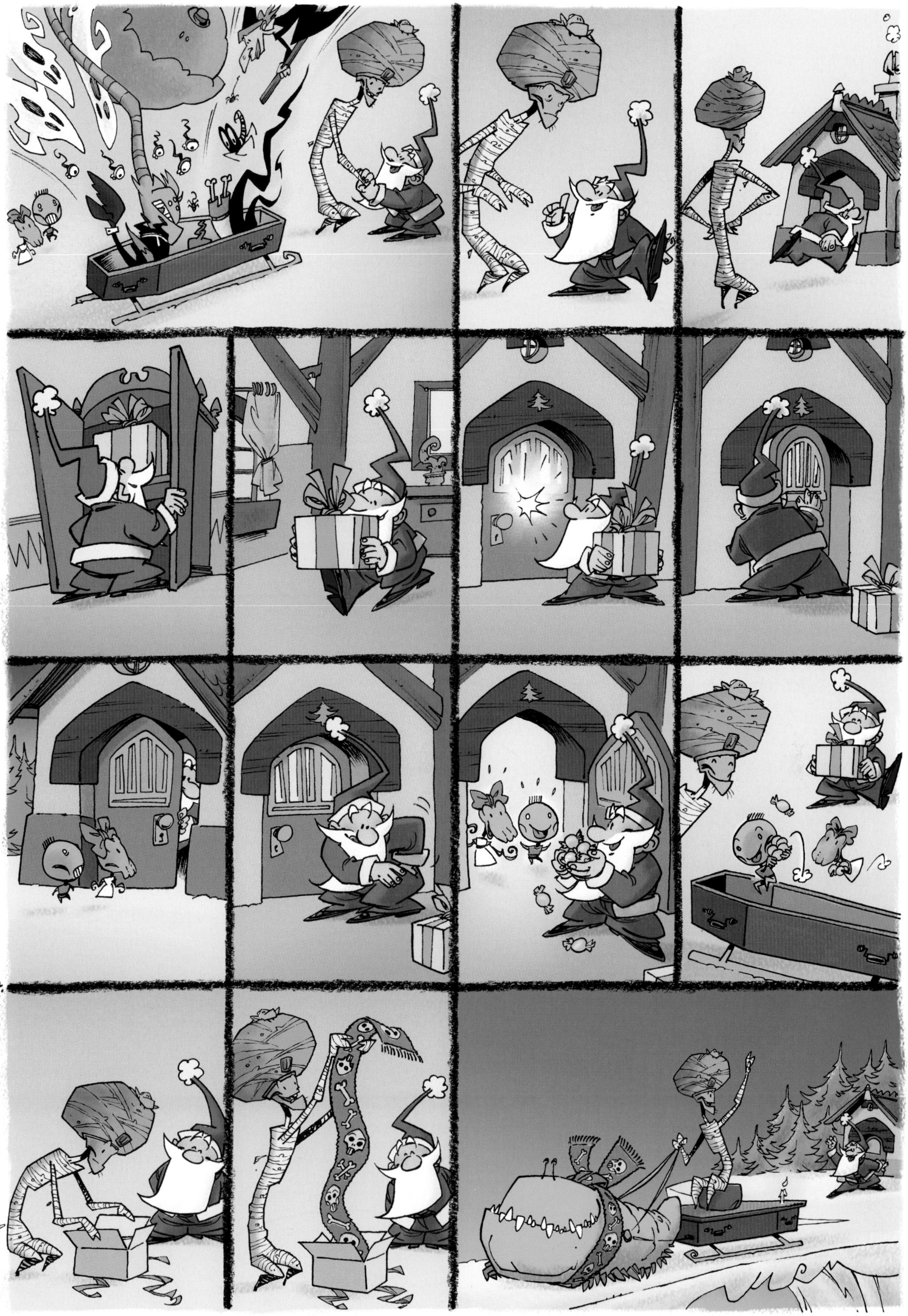

47.

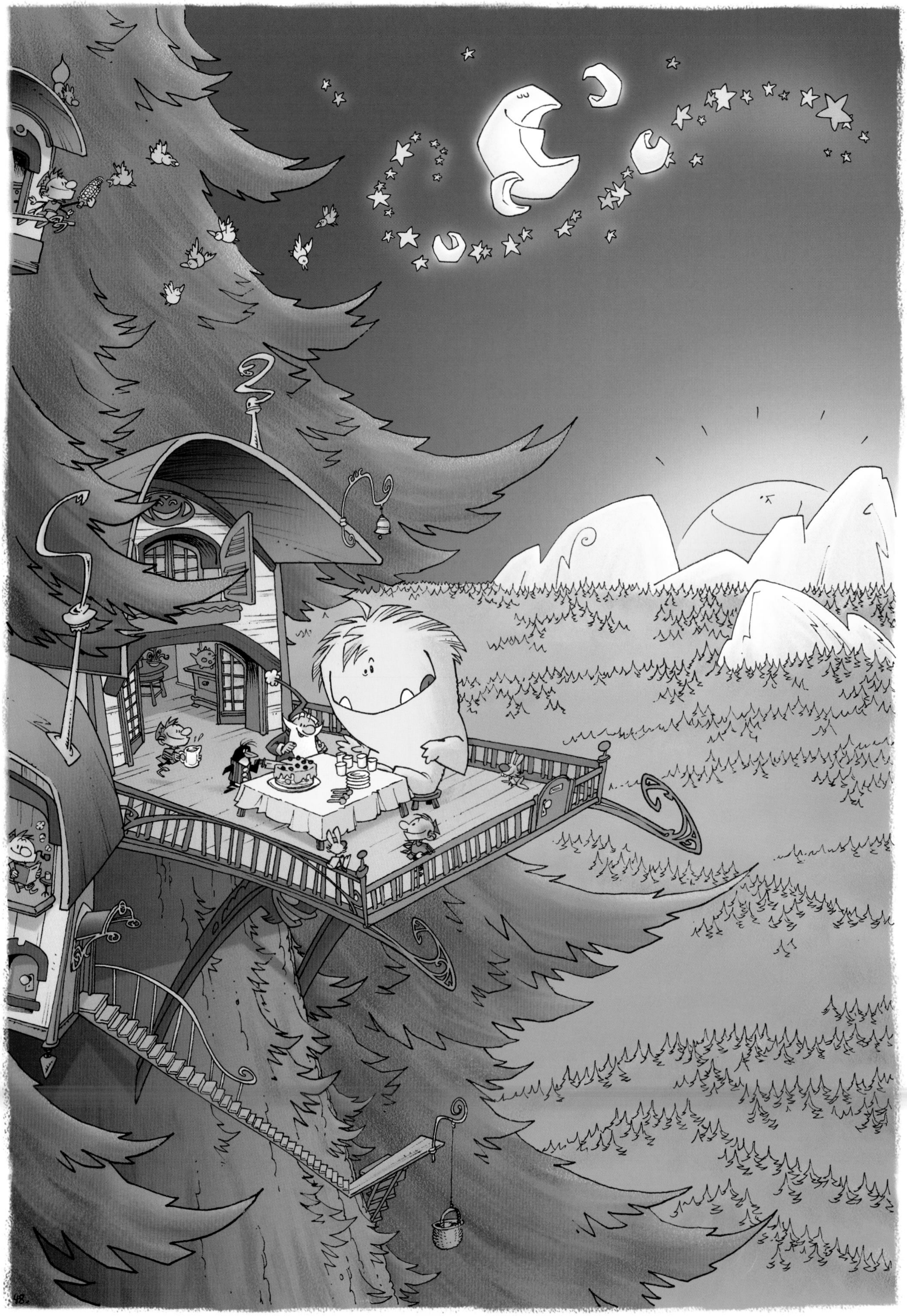

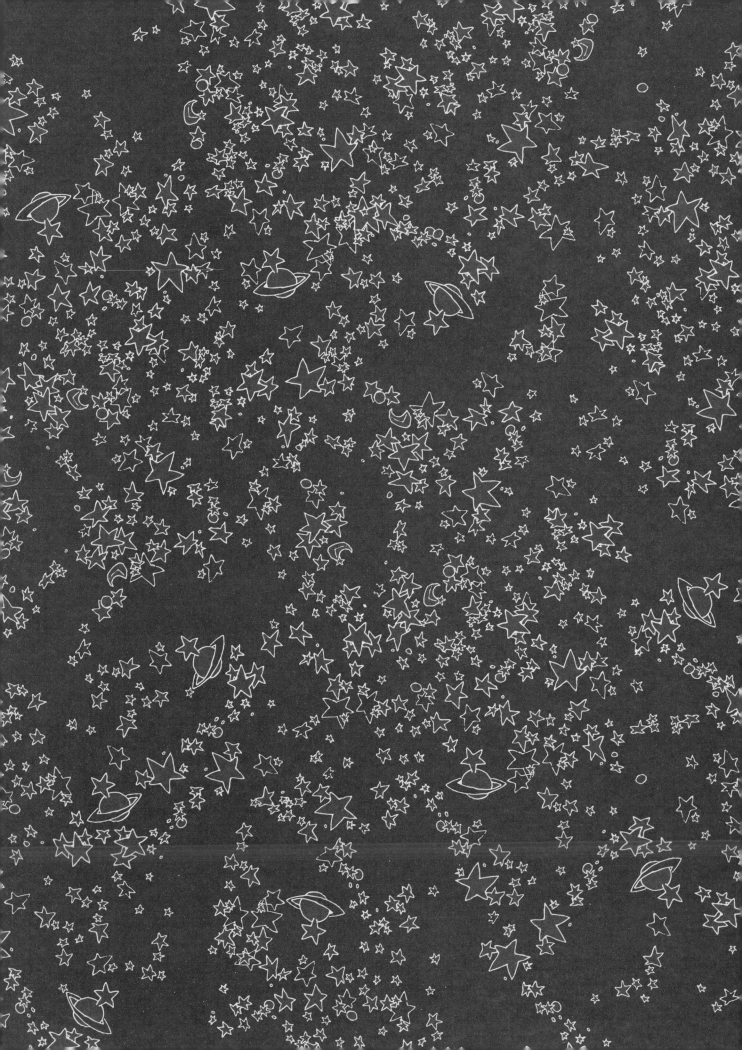